William John Gordon

Under the Avalanche: a Tale of the Sierra Nevada

William John Gordon

Under the Avalanche: a Tale of the Sierra Nevada

ISBN/EAN: 9783743349964

Manufactured in Europe, USA, Canada, Australia, Japa

Cover: Foto ©Andreas Hilbeck / pixelio.de

Manufactured and distributed by brebook publishing software
(www.brebook.com)

William John Gordon

Under the Avalanche: a Tale of the Sierra Nevada

UNDER THE AVALANCHE.

A Tale of the Sierra Nevada.

BY

W. J. GORDON,

AUTHOR OF 'THE KING'S THANE,' ETC. ETC.

LONDON AND NEW YORK:

FREDERICK WARNE AND CO.

1887.

PREFACE.

—o—

I DEDICATE this book to my son FRANK, who, though he is dead, yet lives with me.

I am told it requires a preface. 'It is so very extraordinary!' Perhaps it is. But then the unusual is not necessarily the untrue.

I am certain of one thing; and that is, that the majority of the disbelievers in the lost Kareya will be chiefly those who are unfamiliar with the work of the Geological Survey of California.

W. J. G

CONTENTS.

———o———

UNDER THE AVALANCHE.

CHAPTER I.

DEATH VALLEY.

It was Wednesday, 16th February 1851. The sun was lifting his farewell rays from the eastern slopes of the Sierra del Monte Diablo, as he leisurely dipped behind the woods that crown its ridges. I am not as a rule so particular to date and time; but I have good reasons for remembering that afternoon, and I may as well be

exact when it costs me less effort than to be other-
wise.

As I came up to the front of M'Quarrie's, I found about
a dozen of our fellows crowding round Ned Reid. I had
not seen Ned since we parted at Monterey, seven months
before.

'You must have been told that. You never saw it,'
were the first words I heard.

'It's a fact,' said Ned; 'true as I'm sitting here. They
at first intended to come over by the old Spanish trail;
but, after they passed St. Joseph, they found it running,
as they thought, too much to the south, and so they turned
off and made straight away to the west in a line that took
them through this valley. Well, nothing more was known
of them until a couple of months afterwards, when old
Green came in. He had overheard one redskin telling
another how he had followed the waggon, wondering what
a white caravan was doing in those parts; for, you see, this
valley is a sacred sort of a place among the tribes, and
they all give it a bad name. They say once you are in
you can never get out. That's a fact; and it seemed
Bearspaw made it his business to keep the emigrants in
range, doubtless expecting that if a breakdown happened
there might be some pickings. He followed them to the
Amargosa. To his horror, he saw the waggon begin the
descent. Down the slopes it went to the bottom; but
Bearspaw kept his men on the brink. For the valley is
very steep, like a long crack in the plains, only eight
miles wide. It was a blazing hot day, dry hot, and the
waggon crept more and more slowly across the marsh,
which was all white and shining like silver, with the
white salty stuff that covers it. Soon the waggon stopped;

and the Indians saw the emigrants drop, one after the other—stone dead! Fact! And there was the waggon left standing, and not a sign of life around it. And the Indians did not go down, for they knew they would all meet with the same fate. Not a living thing ever crossed that horrible hole in the plains. You don't believe it? Well, neither did I. And when I heard of it I thought there had been some redskin trickery—as you do, maybe? So, as Druce and I wanted to get back over the Sierra, we made up our minds to follow in the waggon track, and see what we could make of the affair. The track was clear enough, and we followed it until about ten miles from the valley we fell in with Bearspaw and his people. I found Bearspaw rather decent for an Indian. Without being asked, he told us the story of the waggon party and the valley, just as Green had overheard; and when he found we were bound along the same line, he did all he knew to make us cry off—which of course we didn't. Somehow, though, I believed in Bearspaw, by way of a change, and I asked him to go with us. He flatly refused; and it turned out he had never been near the sacred valley since he had seen the emigrants dying around their waggon. The next morning Druce and I left the camp. Bearspaw's son, a little fellow of ten, asked us to take him with us; but his mother would not part with him—and we were not particularly sorry. Old Bearspaw looked very grave when we bade him good-bye; and his last words were, that he had spoken the truth, and that he should never see us again. We soon sighted Death Valley. Beyond were the hills; and we could see the trees thin out, and then all the growth dry up, as the opposite slope lengthened in front of us. Soon the herbage failed altogether; and a barren, lifeless desert lay below. There was nothing but the hummocky rocks, hard and black and glassy, as we afterwards found, the same stuff as they make the stone tools out of—obsidian, I think you call it. The slopes closed in to the northward, where the river entered and was lost, split up into threads which ended in the marsh; for the valley is the sink of the Amargosa. As we neared the descent, Druce exclaimed, "Look! there's the waggon!" And there, the only prominence in the centre of the glittering marsh, was the tilted waggon. And round it, dotted here and there, were a few dull white specks—the bodies of the old man, his wife, and his youngsters. As we reached the edge and looked down, we stood there silent for a time, and then, says Druce, "Blest if it ain't like that old Java yarn of the upas tree." "Yes," says I, "but where's the tree?" For tree there was none. All was dead, and grim, and desolate, and unearthly-like!'

'Drive on, Ned! Never mind the scenery,' said the Scotchman. 'Did the bodies have their heads on?'

' Yes.'

' And the scalps on.'

' Yes.'

' Do you mean to say there were no tomahawk marks? or didn't you go near enough to see?'

' Well, I'll tell you what I did see. I saw a flock of birds coming like a cloud from the snowy slopes of the Sierra. I saw that cloud grow larger as it neared us. I saw it seek to cross the valley, and when it reached the centre I saw the birds drop in dozens, dead and dying, on the glittering salt.'

' Oh, all right, Ned! that'll do!' came in chorus from the circle.

'It is the truth! Ned Reid speaks truth!' said the Barber.

Who was the Barber? There now, I ought to have begun with him, for he is the most important personage in this story. Had it not been for him, I should never have written this truthful chronicle of the strangest experience of my life. He was an Indian—one of the Digger Indians, as the redskins to the west of the Rockies are called by the Californians. But he was the finest representative of his race I ever met. He was six feet two if he was an inch, well built, lithe, and sinewy, with every muscle duly and proportionately developed. Broad-browed, straight-nosed, large-eyed, and firm-lipped, it seemed almost an insult to class him with the miserable, shambling, undersized creatures whose doom is unmistake-able. The Barber was a mystery. I had met him about two months before, and M'Quarrie had taken him on as an extra hand; and since, without a single relapse, he had kept steadily at work, doing as much in a day as any half-dozen of the ordinary redskins. M'Quarrie was nearly always growling at his men; but he had no com-plaint to make of the Barber. 'If my nose,' said the old man, 'didn't tell me different, I could swear he was an Aberdeenshire man that had got copperwashed!' 'Too good to last!' was the general verdict. So said the whites, and so, curiously enough, said the Indians, who all fought shy of him.

'It is true! Ned Reid speaks truth,' said the Barber.

'Eh? hallo! what do you know about it?' said Reid.

'I speak the truth,' said the Indian.

'They all do,' sneered Lacroix.

'I'll go bail he does,' said I.

'My goodness!' said Reid. 'Why, how are you, Langham? Fancy you being here! Why, when I left you at Monterey, I thought you had said good-bye to your ship, to make your fortune in a fortnight. What have you been doing? What are you doing here on the San Joaquin? Didn't the Grass Valley spec come off?'

'I'll tell you all about that, Ned, another time. But I want to hear the rest of this Death Valley business. What are you driving at?'

'Oh, a most curious place it is, but these fellows won't believe it. You don't seem to have learnt much if you go bail for a Digger.'

'You believed in Bearspaw, and I believe in the Barber. We both of us think there are exceptions to every rule, and these are the exceptions.'

'Well, then,' said Ned, 'perhaps the exception will tell us what he knows of the Death Valley, for I think my part of the story will come in best at the finish. I say, mister, how do you know I'm telling the truth?'

The Barber seemed inclined to sulk.

'Have you been in the valley?' asked M'Quarrie.

'I have,' said the Indian.

'Then there's one that got out of it,' broke in Lacroix.

'Perhaps the Digger is the Scot that M'Quarrie says he is, and the silvery salt discoloured him.'

'Tell us what you know,' said I.

'I crossed the Snowy Mountains,' said the Barber. 'and I camped on the Amargosa. I followed it till it entered the valley, and I kept on the western side, and camped among the giant rocks, a day's journey along the brink. And, as I journeyed to the south, I looked over the Valley of Death, and I saw across it on the distant plains a slowly moving speck. I waited and watched, and the speck, as it grew nearer, became a waggon. I saw the waggon crawl down the opposite slope to the barren marsh below. As it reached the level, deep down, deeper down than the western sea, two birds flew eastwards from behind me. As they reached the middle of the marsh, they fluttered and fell and died. And as the waggon reached the springs of salt, its wheels ran ever more slowly, until they stopped, and I saw the old chief and his wife and little ones die there under the poisonous breath of the silvery flower. It is a sacred place, a place where a man can die of thirst while water is within his reach. I tried to go down to help, but my breath grew thick and my throat was parched, and I knew I could do no good by crawling into the Valley of Death.'

'What did you do then?' asked Ned.

'I went away for a time, but I returned, and the waggon was there, and the dead were there drying in the sun, for no wind ever blows and no rain ever falls to hide what is laid on the bed of salt.'

'What were you doing there, Barber?'

The Indian made no reply. Reid looked at him keenly and then continued.

'Anyhow what he says is quite right, though he hasn't backed up my bird story. We did see the birds, as Druce will tell you; and, thinking of the upas tree, we resolved to get down into the valley by easy stages, one of us going first, so that we could help each other if necessary. Now it was much colder then than it had been when the waggon went, and as Druce said the Upas Valley was not so bad in the winter time, so this proved to be. We got on very well, but the air was very dry, and the water we drank seemed to do us no good. We struggled on half-suffocated. We reached the waggon and gave one look in, and then the atmosphere nearly did for us. Druce snatched up a water-flask, and started to run back, but before he had gone a dozen yards he fainted. I picked him up and ran with him in my arms. As the ground rose I felt the air get fresher; and, running round on to the top of a projecting rock, I rested. The rock was different to all the others I had seen. They were black; this was a brilliant green. I started again, and got Druce safely up, and he revived. The bodies and the waggon were untouched; there was not the slightest sign of plunder or violence. All seemed to have been choked in the poison-cloud. In the water-flask there was a pint of water, so that it was not for want of water that its owner died. We camped on the plain that night, and in the early morning took another good look into the valley. The rock on which I had rested with Druce caught my attention, and I made a rapid run down to it and knocked off a piece as a keepsake. Seems to me it's a jewellery kind of a thing. What do you think?'

And from his pouch Reid brought forth a small piece of jade, which he handed round.

'I don't think much of that,' said Lacroix.

Neither did any one else except the Indian, who turned it over and over, and weighed it in his hand, and finally gave it a lick to bring out its colour.

'Did you get this on the east or the west of the valley?' he asked.

'On the east,' said Reid. 'But why?'

'Rock like this on the west,' said the Indian.

'Perhaps so,' said Lacroix; 'green on both sides.' The Barber handed back the stone and left us; and Reid rose saying,—

'I have said my say now. Let me hear the best news from you.'

The story of the valley seemed soon forgotten in the general conversation that ensued. When the time arrived to turn in, Reid became my guest, and I took him off with me to my hut, which was a little apart from the other buildings.

'What made you leave Grass Valley?' asked Ned.

'Because I was a fool,' said I. 'When I left the *Monmouth* with the others, I found my way there, fell into luck, and was doing well. But one day Crowther, who had been our boatswain's mate, turned up and showed me an old piece of paper he had swapped from some Indian, and which stated that one of the tributaries of the San Joaquin had a bed of golden pebbles, and that the farther you followed the torrent up into the mountains, the thicker lay the gold. There was a smack of pro- bability about the idea, and Crowther persuaded me to join him in the search. And off we went for the stream with the golden gravel. We crossed a good many streams, as you may imagine, but we did not happen to hit on the right one, and we even got as far as Lake Tulare, where Jim got a "whisper." He was always getting whispers. This particular whisper was about a quicksilver hill—a cinnabar deposit, I suppose. We parted company the best of friends, he going south to his cinnabar, leaving me in sole possession of the paper that had sent us off on our wild-goose chase.'

'There's nothing impossible in that gold gravel notion,'

said Ned. 'There are stranger things than that in California. But how came you here?'

'On my way back I met M'Quarrie, who turned out to be a cousin of mine, and he asked me to join him for a month or so. The gold-washing doesn't seem up to much, but the farming promises well, and I am not sure it isn't the best game of the two.'

'It won't suit you for long yet awhile, though,' said Ned. 'And now, who's our friend the big Barber, and where did he get his name from?'

'His name was given him by M'Quarrie when he took him on. It was for some facetious reason, but I forget what now. I know nothing about him, except that he has always been truthful and trustworthy, which very few Indians are. He seems to me to be quite a superior fellow to the rest, and I like his look. I feel sure he has got a history. I met him the day before I came across M'Quarrie. He had asked me to give him a job. I recommended him, and he has really worked well.'

'I don't believe in Diggers,' said Ned, 'and I should keep an eye on the Barber.'

'I suppose it's all true about that Death Valley?'

'What I told you was true, every word of it. But was it all true what your Digger told us?'

CHAPTER II.

Was it all true that the Digger had told us ? How strange that he of all men in the world should have been wandering on the other side of the Sierra, and camping by the Valley of Death !

Reid I knew as a truthful man, much given to the marvellous ; a man of a restless spirit, impatient of the authority of those he failed to respect, who had taken to the woods in search of the freedom he never found ; a shrewd, determined man, clean and ready in thought and speech, with a cynical crust of inconsiderable thickness. In fact, the more I knew him,— and I was now to know him well,—the more I liked him. But the Barber ? I lay and thought ; and thought and dozed ; and dozed and slept. I was just journeying back to consciousness, and fancying I must be awake, when I was startled out of dreamland with,—

'Wake up there!   The horses are stolen!'

'Early morning intelligence with a vengeance!' said I. In a minute Reid was out of the hut, and ready for action. I followed.

Two men had just ridden in to bring us the news of our disaster.   It seemed absurd to thus learn from others what we should have been the first to find out for ourselves, but, as Fielden said, 'circumstances were agin us.'   We could see the tracks of the horses leading down the knoll and through the paddock, between the Wakalla and the Dandy, as we called the streamlet which joined the San Joaquin about a mile to the south.   But, half-way across, the tracks faded off with the field into the morning haze; and by the side of the fence in the foreground lay poor Sam, who had evidently caught sight of the thieves, and been cut down from behind as he was about to give the alarm.   Where was our other guard?   He could not be found.   The Barber had vanished.

Fortunately Sam was not dead.

'They were in too much of a hurry,' said Ned, as he bent over him.   'Knocked him senseless, perhaps knocked him silly; that's all.   He'll be better soon.   You leave him to me.'

And, while Ned was busy doing his best to revive him, we others, at M'Quarrie's request, set about getting breakfast.

'Can't gain anything by being in a hurry,' said the old man.   'Let us take it coolly, and talk it over.   Perhaps Sam will throw some light on the subject.'

'Don't think he'll throw much,' said Caffrey, one of

the new-comers. 'You'll find they were too quick for him.'

And so it proved. When Sam returned to consciousness, all he could report was that he had received a terrific blow on the back of his head at the same moment as a mounted Indian rode out from the shadow of the house.

'Thought so,' said Caffrey. 'All you'll know is what I told you—until you catch them.'

'Well, let's have your story in full, then.' And, thus invited, Caffrey, a sandy, thickset, keen-eyed, active little man, proceeded to relate how he and his lanky friend, 'Crane' Smith, had been camping out the previous night four miles away up the Wakalla.

'We kept a look-out,' said he, 'as we always do, talk as they may about these honest Indians. Well, sir, it was six o'clock, there or thereabouts, and I was sitting over the fire, looking at old Smith snoozing away at his ease. And I was thinking of nothing in particular, and feeling somehow that something was going to happen, when, sir, I felt a rope slip over my neck. "Lassoed, by jingo!" thought I quick as a flash. And, snatching out my revolver, I swung round to fire, and the rope tightened as I did so. And, sir, I didn't fire,'—and Caffrey drawled out his jerky sentences most provokingly,—'I didn't fire. I was too much astonished. The Indian was too big. I could just see him in the firelight looking calmly down on me. Luckily I didn't let fly; for the Indian, sir, was my old horse Pedro; and the rope I thought was a lasso was merely his lariat, which in the course of his wandering round the fire he had dragged over my neck. It ain't so pleasant to feel a rope where your collar ought to be, and I can tell you I came over queer at first—I did that;

but when I saw old Ped looking so serious at me, I burst
out laughing; and up jumped Smith, wideawake as usual
when a joke was going. Well, we were chuckling over
my scare, and I was just giving the fire a stir, when we
were dead silent for a moment, and we heard a faint
thirrup, thirrup, thirrup. "Horses!" hissed Smith.
"Robbery!" said I, and we were in cover in a jiffey. Closer
and closer came the row, and in the first streak or two of
the daylight we saw as they dashed past some forty red-
skinned rascals; fine, tall fellows, a size or two larger than
the plains Diggers. They had about a dozen led horses,
on one of which was strapped a chap who seemed to be a
prisoner and kept in the thick of them. We thought it
best to be quiet; we could do no good, and horses can't
go very far up these hills at that rate. And so we agreed
our best plan was to hurry in here and see what you were
doing, and if you think it worth while to follow the trail
we'll join—if agreeable.'

'I'll make one,' said Reid.

'I'll go, of course,' said Lacroix, 'and I'll put a bullet
through the Barber. It's easy to see what his game was.
It's the same as Carson told us about the Indian that cut
from Robidoux. He came here as a spy, and brought his
friends down when he was sure of the game. He gave
Sam his knock, and cleared off in proper Indian style.'

'Then, sir, who was the prisoner?' asked Caffrey.

'The Barber,' said I; 'they nailed him, gagged him, and
carried him off.'

'Ask Sam if he saw anything of the Barber,' said
M'Quarrie.

Sam had seen and heard nothing.

'If your Indian is a scoundrel,' said Reid, 'he ought to

be followed and shot. If he is innocent, and has been carried off a prisoner, he ought to be followed and freed. Anyhow, the horses were stolen, and the thieves ought to suffer. What do you think, Langham? Innocent or guilty, follow we must.'

I need scarcely say we agreed to follow immediately, if we could only borrow sufficient horses or mules. Little did we suspect where the chase would lead us. Altogether those willing to go numbered eleven. Six of us— Reid, Lacroix, Fielden, M'Quarrie, Caffrey, and the Crane —were hardy, experienced backwoodsmen, equal to any fortune in any position on any of the hills or plains. The rest were jacks-of-all-trades and rovers in general, all very eager for the chase, and all untried in Indian warfare. I was quite a raw hand at such work,—a young fellow of two-and-twenty, escaped from the sea, as it turned out merely for a few months, in the hope of making a sudden fortune by finding a nugget or stumbling on a mine. As I look back, it seems to me that the only qualification I possessed was inordinate self-confidence.

By ten o'clock we had mustered enough horses, and were off. Each of us was armed with rifle and revolver; most of us boasted a long hunting-knife. I had no knife, but took what the others did not—an extra revolver. We of course did not leave the station deserted. When we sent round Smith and Caffrey with the news, and borrowed our mounts, we had arranged for our neighbours to see that all went well in our absence and to forward assistance if necessary. We were confident that the horses could not have gone very far up the hills, and expected to recover them after a short, sharp, and futile resistance.

Off we went, across the paddock and along the fringe

of the woods where Caffrey and the Crane had camped, and seen the thieves go by. M'Quarrie's looked pleasant enough in the morning sun, but we had few thoughts to spare on it. As we glanced down from the eastern slope, the broad stream of the San Joaquin, with its many feeders joining it at right angles, lay spread out like a silver tree on an emerald field. To our left, the tiny Dandy went flowing in from its source in the adjoining woods; to our right the noisy Wakalla went glittering past after its long troubled journey from the distant mountains. From those deeply snow-capped heights its restless waters had leapt rather than run, for the cascades in its course we were to count by the dozen as it cut down into the rocky ribs of the Sierra Nevada, and cleft its stairway through the foot hills. All the way up the river seemed to be branchless. There were no side streams parallel to the San Joaquin. The Wakalla derived all its waters from the snowfield, and, retaining its width for miles and miles, swept on recklessly to join the chief Californian river. There was no difficulty as to the trail; the prints of the horses' hoofs were too clear to be mistaken. Till now they led us by the river, and then, making a wide sweep to take advantage of the better ground, they again neared the bank, and then, seemingly for good, trended off to the south-east. On we went without a check until we pulled up to rest. Then we went on again, and all that afternoon, until the sun went down, we continued the chase—in vain. Caffrey and the Crane rode ahead to reconnoitre, but found no trace of the enemy or of the trail coming to an end. And we camped for the night.

By daybreak we were up and stirring, and as soon as the sun rose we were off. Reid went on in advance, followed by Caffrey, and to these two we trusted to keep us out of ambush. The trail took us again to the river, and then again through a tongue of woodland out on to a narrow open plain with trees again beyond. As we trotted from under shelter, we saw our advance guard about half a mile ahead halted on a gentle rise that ran across the plateau. And almost immediately afterwards Reid turned his horse's head and rode towards us.

'Found!' said he, as he came up. 'They are just over the ridge there in those trees, and seem to think we are coming. They are saddling their horses, and getting ready for a start.'

'How many are there?'

'I counted fifty, but I don't think they have any guns.'

'What are they?'

'Caffrey says they are the same as he saw; but they are a big lot of fellows, quite different to the usual run of Indians this side of the Sierra.'

'Like the Barber?'

'Something, but not so well built, and they don't look as big. I expect we shall find it a tough job.'

'Are our horses there?'

'Mine is. I can't swear to yours, though I have no doubt you'll find them. But, anyhow, there are more horses than the beggars want, and we may as well have them.'

All this time we had been approaching the ridge. When we had nearly reached it, Caffrey beckoned us to stop, and came and joined us.

We held a council of war. The council was of an unusual kind. Unlike most such councils, we intended to fight, and ended by fighting; still more unlike such councils, one man had a plan which was approved the instant it was explained; and, even still more unlike such councils, the plan did not want much explanation, for it was suggested by the ablest, understood by the dullest, and adopted unanimously in rather less than three minutes. It was Caffrey's plan, and to him belongs the honour of the victory—a very barren victory, as it proved.

We left M'Quarrie and two men to take charge of the horses and form the reserve. Caffrey, Smith, Fielden, and Lacroix went off to the right, so as to attack the Indians on the flank. We others followed them to the ridge, and then, plunging into the trees in front of us, went straight at the right corner of the Indian camp.

Caffrey fired the first shot, and an Indian fell. Springing behind the trees, the redskins were instantly at work, and arrow after arrow came whistling past. While we were loading, at least a score of arrows could be rained off; and very alarming the long shafts proved to me, as with each flutter of the bowstrings they floated spitefully towards us, and quivered in the tree-trunks, or buried themselves in the ground. The course of a bullet no man can follow, but an arrow is a messenger of death whose whole journey is visible.

Very uncomfortable I felt at first, and for a long time I did not shoot. It was only when I found a fellow aiming deliberately at me that I recognised it was necessary for me to fire if I wished to live. I fired, and the man fell; and then I felt as though a skin had been drawn off me, and I fought like the rest.

From tree to tree we advanced, and from tree to tree

we slowly drove the Diggers. They were seven to one, and the rapidity of their shooting gave them an advantage, which, however, the shelter of the trees rendered of little use. Ably led, they suddenly took the offensive. Nearer and nearer, dodging from trunk to trunk, they came. Waiting their chance until nearly all our rifles were unloaded, they gave a terrific whoop, and charged right on to us. Alas for their hopes! Our rifles, as they judged, were useless; but they knew `nothing of our revolvers, and, as soon as we had them well within pistol range, we greeted them with a rattling fire that sent them staggering to the trees. Back they went, fighting every inch of the way. At last they reached a mass of boulders and rugged rocks hidden among thick underwood. There it was that the real battle began. All the rest we found was merely an opening skirmish.

Some twenty of the enemy had fallen, wounded or killed; but all of them had been carried out of fire, and the horses had all been led to the rear. The rough ground lay in a half-moon; we could not work round it. All we could do was to press the attack in front. None of our men had been seriously injured, though Fielden and the Crane had received slight flesh-wounds.

As the Indians disappeared under cover of the rocks, Reid and I found ourselves loading behind two neighbouring trees. Ned was the picture of steadiness; he was as cool as if he were amusing himself shooting at a mark.

'Seen the Barber yet?' he asked.

'No. These fellows seem to belong to a different tribe.'

'If he helped to steal the horses, he'll be in the fight round those rocks.'

'The horses have gone.'

'Only to the rear, I think. This is a queer business. I fancy we shan't all see the end.'

'There's one won't. Look!'

Lacroix had fallen. His foot had caught in a twig, and as he stumbled forward an arrow whipped through his hunting-shirt and pinned him to the ground. Instantly half a dozen of the redskins left their cover. Tomahawk on high, they leapt yelling towards him. The leader had nearly reached the unhappy trapper, when Reid's rifle rose to its work, and, as the white puff thinned away, the victim stooped quite double, and fell forward—dead. The others turned to shelter, and Lacroix was saved— only for a time.

Never shall I forget that desperate fight among the rocks. Soon I found myself on one side of a boulder, with an Indian on the other watching my every move- ment. It was to be his life or mine. There was no escape for both of us; he who made the first slip would fall. The Digger watched me, and I watched him. Not for an instant did we take our eyes off each other. Every twitch and promise of movement did we follow and guard, as we blinked and glared, and strove to read each other's innermost thought. A horrible fascination came over me. I felt as if my power of will was slipping away. It seemed to me hours since the horrible gaze began. I knew that I should fail and die unless some one intervened. Fortunately help did come; and my antagonist was the first that fell as M'Quarrie brought up the reserve.

As it was with me, so it was with the others. Every rock was the scene of a lengthened duel fought within arrowshot of the rear-guard, who every now and then joined in the fray. From rock to tree, from tree to bush, from bush to rock again we drove the enemy, and at last the arrow rain ceased. We were engaged only with those immediately in front of us. Lacroix fell shot through the heart. Fielden sold his life dearly, and lay clasped in the death embrace of the man who gave him his last wound. Peters dropped, crushed lifeless with a stone hurled full in his face.

Reid and the long-legged Crane were farthest in advance. Caffrey and I came next. The others were a few yards behind, giving help where required. The noise of the fight had almost ceased, for each of us was left with only one antagonist barring the way to the crest of the ridge. Reid was the first to clear away the danger. The Indian thought a chance had come, and let fly an arrow, which Ned warded off with his revolver as he aimed and fired. Hearing the death-yell, and seeing that the odds were hopelessly against them, the three survivors gave a terrific shout, and boldly rushed to close with us. We gave them no chance. They met their fate. We stepped over them, and ran to see what had become of their companions.

They had all disappeared. The heap of rocks was on the edge of a deep gully that curved away to the eastward. We looked down it in vain for the fugitives. Our horses were as far off as ever. The only Indians near were those lying dead in the wood among the rocks.

CHAPTER III.

THE GOLDEN GRAVEL.

HOULD we follow?

We looked to Caffrey, who had acted as our commander-in-chief.

'Well?' said M'Quarrie to him.

'Well,' sir, said Caffrey, 'what I want to know is where those rascals come from. Where have they gone to? I have spent many a year on the Pacific slope south and west of this, but never did I see Diggers like those chaps, or heard of a Digger making such a fight. Away to the east there's nothing but snow at this time. They cannot cross the Cascade Range. There's no place for them hereabouts that I know of.'

'Let's follow them and see,' said Ned.

'Follow them?—yes. But are we strong enough? If they fight like that away from home, they'll fight as well when their squaws are by. We've lost three of our best men, and we shall be less in number, while they are more. They can't go north, they can't go south, they can't get over the range. They must live somewhere not far up the hills, and can be easily found when we want them. Let us send back for help, and stay here till we get a dozen more men. Then we can find and follow the trail with some chance of winning.'

'It's best so, I'm afraid,' said M'Quarrie.

'I'll be off and hurry them up,' said Smith. 'What says Mr. Reid?'

'Mr. Reid says, never lose scent of a redskin when he's on the run. This affair is a mystery to me. The men we've been fighting are not of the same tribe as the Barber belonged to. Their marks were different, and their twang was different. Where he came from I don't know; where he has gone to I don't know. He wasn't in the fight. If he was the prisoner, they have nobbled him for some purpose of their own. Where has my horse gone? I am not going to let old Zeke be spirited away by some fellows from the moon in this fashion without knowing the reason why. You stay here and send for help, as Caffrey says. I'll follow on and keep out of shot, and when you come up I can be of use.'

'I'll go with you,' said I.

'What! you, eh? Well, two heads are better than one. But there'll be a little risk.'

'Never mind the risk. I'm willing to share that with you, if you don't object.'

'Better stay here and go on with us,' said Caffrey.

'No,' replied Ned. 'I think not. You be as quick as you can, and I'll trust to you to come to my assistance.'

And, in short, Ned and I filled up with stores and ammunition and started down the gully. It curved away to the eastward, as I have said, and we were soon out of sight of our companions. The track was obvious enough. It led along the bottom, and rose to the level of the plain among a patch of forest some two miles from the scene of our recent fight. Through the forest we went, out into the open. Then we entered another patch of woodland, and, following the trail to the north, found it was leading us to the river.

'We are sure to end on a river of some sort,' said Ned. 'If these horse-stealers are Californians, they are bound to have their village by the side of a stream.'

'Why?'

'All the Diggers do. Other Indians have their villages on the hill-tops.'

'Why do you call them Diggers? Is that their right name?'

'They call them Diggers because they dig. They mostly live on roots and corn, and are farmers, in fact, in a small way. Some folks say they never touch animal food, but I know better. What their real name is I don't know for certain. I fancy it is Mutsun, or some such word.'

'That doesn't sound right to me.'

'Well, perhaps not. I only heard the word once. However, perhaps your barbering friend will tell us if we find him.'

'Do you think he was a spy?'

'Can't say,' said Reid. 'I only saw him for that few minutes the night before last. You knew him, and you say you would trust him. I wouldn't trust an Indian, but I would trust your judgment. You are too green to go far wrong. You don't judge from your experience, only from your fancies. You are like the women, who are generally right because they know so little.'

'They have a different sort of knowledge, you mean.'

'That's better. And it's an older knowledge. It isn't dotted out into because and because, and therefore and nevertheless, and all that sort of thing. A man says another's a bad un because he does this, and because he does that; whereas a girl gives him a look, and says he's a bad un because he's a bad un—and there's an end of it.'

'You are not a woman-hater, then, like most of you fellows.'

'Not I; but then they never say I'm a bad un,' said Ned, with a grin. 'They play one game; we play another. Our game's a good one if we know all about it, which we don't. Their game's not so good, perhaps, but it must have been played longest. The mother's habit is the daughter's nature. When Bearspaw was telling me about the waggon in the Death Valley, he evidently was puzzled as to why the emigrants went there. Not so his squaw. Her answer was ready enough. "Him fool!" When I asked why Bearspaw hadn't gone down for the guns, "Him not fool!" was her remark. When I said I was going down she looked a bit staggered, but seemed to have no fears for my safety. Bearspaw thought I was

committing suicide, and gave me his last good-bye. Mrs.
Bearspaw very civilly said, "Him no fool!" and hoped I
would call in next time I passed. Now, according to his
lights, Bearspaw was right; but he did not know everything. He knew that no one who had been there before
had come back, and therefore, and therefore, and so on.
Mrs. Bearspaw didn't worry about the reasoning, but got
to the grit of the matter at once. It was nothing to her
that no one she had heard of had come back.'

'But somebody had. How about the Barber?'

'Ah!' said Reid; 'that's what I thought. But "him
no fool," though he may be a shameless rascal.'

As we neared the river we heard the roar of falling
water. The trail followed the brink of the canyon, and
as we passed we could look down to the eddying stream
beneath. The walls were nearly vertical, rising sheer
from the very bottom. At the far end they closed in
somewhat more than the perspective seemed to justify.
There a lofty cascade curved over in one solid mass, like
a thick roll of glass. The sunlight just fell on the brawl-
ing upper river. Ruled off by the shadow from the silver
ripples, the smooth fall was almost invisible until it poured
into its foam-cloud below. And from the cloud there
broke forth a shower of spurts and patches that floated
on the swirling waves, and danced and vanished down
the gloomy gorge. As soon as we were abreast of the
fall, we found another stretch of the river, ended by
another waterfall about a mile ahead. Then the walls
began to widen as we descended a long hill slope, and
then the river ran for several hundred yards along a
channel thickly strewn with great rock masses that broke
it up into a thousand rills. During that afternoon, as we

followed the canyon bank, we passed sixteen different cascades and four long stretches of rapids.

At last we reached a wide, rolling country. The stream flowed more quietly. The canyon came to an end. And at a spot where the stream was almost level with the banks the trail split. The main trail, the one we had been following, went off abruptly to the right; but straight ahead there went another and older trail, leading apparently to a camp or village from which Ned declared he could see smoke rising. I looked where he pointed, and, steadily gazing for a moment or so, I saw a puff rise and float over the trees.

'We must leave the river,' said Ned. 'If we go wrong we can start fresh from here.'

We turned our backs to the Wakalla and struck due south. The trail led us into a patch of woodland, and there, for us, it ended. The air had been gradually growing colder, the clouds had been banking up as the rising wind brought them off the hills. Suddenly the sun was obscured, and we were caught in a heavy snowstorm. In the patch the Indians had evidently halted, and, before we could find by which side they left it, the snow had covered the ground.

'I can't bring myself to think that this trail goes far from the river,' said Ned. 'It ought to get back there somehow. And as we can do no good here we might as well make for the smoke. This snow will soon blow over, but it will take till next morning to melt.'

To the smoke we steered. Before we reached it we were again on the bank of the Wakalla, rising again to some height above the stream, and crowned with trees. Through the trees we went, and before us, by the side of

a low waterfall, a few furlongs off, lay an Indian settlement.   Evidently it was a peaceful and prosperous one.
The storm had ceased, the sun had come forth again, and
the huts looked quite homelike in the rosy snow.

'Well, captin, how goes it?'

We instinctively felt for our revolvers as a tall young
Indian stepped towards us from behind one of the trees
The snow all round was untrodden.   He had evidently
been there for some time.

'Wumeh?' said Reid; 'whence come you?'

The seeming savage laughed.

'Me understand English better than you speak
Choomteya.'

'That's the word you wanted,' said Reid to me.   'The
Diggers hereabouts are Choomteyas, a tribe of the Mee-
wocs.'   And then, turning to the Indian, he continued,
'Who are you?'

'I am Ahrua, the son of Taipoksee.   Who are you?
Do you come to seek gold?'

'Yes, if you have any to spare,' said Ned.   'How much
have you?'

'I will lead you to my father.'

'You are quite a man of business,' said I.

'Business to business men,' said Ahrua.

We stared at him.   Could this scantily - clothed son
of the wilderness be some office - boy escaped from
'Frisco?

'Where do you get your gold from?' asked Reid.

'In the morning you will see.   It grows in the gravel
of the stream.'

'Hullo!' said Ned; 'where's that bit of paper of yours?
Isn't this your golden gravel?'

Ahrua understood at least the latter part of the question.

'The golden gravel is not his, but my father's. Nowhere is gold got as my father gets it. He is the friend of the white man, and the terror of the Awahnees.'

'Who are the Awahnees?' asked I.

'They are the men of the mountains, who would steal if they dared.'

'Steal horses?' asked Reid.

'Steal everything!' said the Indian, with a sigh, as if he regretted he could not say the same of himself. 'They are tall and mighty; they have bows and arrows; but Tenaya is no match for Taipoksee. We are peaceful Indians. We have much gold.'

Ahrua announced the fact with as much complacency as if he were a city merchant with a five-figure balance at his bankers.

'Have the Awahnees been past here lately?' asked Ned.

'My father will tell you.'

'We must see the old gentleman,' said I.

'Yes,' said Ned, 'and ask him about that gravel.'

We were led to the 'palace,' and introduced to the great chief. Great chief he really was, as we afterwards learned; and no better ruler can the Choomteyas boast. When he died, six years after our visit, there were twelve hundred men present at his funeral,—an enormous number for such a communistic nation as the Meewocs. Fortunately he was friendly. He had found that the whites sought gold for the comfort it enabled them to purchase, and, being himself in possession of an ample source of the precious metal, he worked it in his own peculiar way, and

held his land against all comers. He was the richest
Indian I ever met,—much too rich to engage in reckless
fighting. But he was a splendid fighter and leader when
he did begin ; and, careless as he seemed, was always
prepared for eventualities. Within a few minutes of our
reception, we found that he had had us under observation
for several miles.

We told him why we followed the trail, and how we
lost it.

' Beware of the Awahnees,' said he. ' Seek them not
in their home until another moon has passed.'

' They stole our horses,' said Reid.

' If you follow them now you will be lost.'

' Where do the Awahnees live ? '

' Their home is on the banks of the river whose music
you hear, but it is high up among the mountains.'

' So I thought,' said Reid. ' But how far off is it ? '

' A four days' journey, but not by the stream.'

' Why not ? '

' There is no way for a man to pass. To follow the
Awahnees you must turn to the south or the north, and
not regain the Wakalla till far above this.'

' Then the thieves will escape us.'

' No,' said Taipoksee. ' There is no need of haste.
The Awahnees will be found when you want them.
Their home will not change until the winter comes
again.'

Thus far Taipoksee had been as stiff and ceremonious
as could reasonably be expected of a man in his exalted
position. But politics soon grew irksome to him, a
change set in, and he thawed into commerce.

' Ahrua says you wish to buy gold.'

'Quite a mistake,' said Reid; 'we thought we would take any you might have to spare.'

'At how much?' said the chief. 'Our gold is good, and it always brings a good price.'

'Do you sell it, then?'

'Sell to those that will buy.'

'Do people come here for it?'

'No, but every moon my young men carry it to the banker.'

'Do you mean to say you have a regular monthly gold escort?'

'It is so,' said Taipoksee. And it was so, as we afterwards found.

'Where does the gold come from?'

'From the bed of the Wakalla.'

'From under the water?'

'Yes. To-morrow you will see.'

'We are on the track of the golden gravel, I believe,' said Ned to me, as we turned in for the night in a wigwam which the hospitable old fellow had put at our disposal. 'We are in for three finds now. First, to find old Zeke; second, to find that rascally Barber; third, to find your fortune. Does Crowther hold shares in the gravel pit?'.

'No. It's all mine—when I find it.'

'When you get it, you mean. I'll stand in for a tenth, if you've no objection.'

'Oh, more than that! Let us agree you are to have Crowther's half.'

'Done! Queer old boy, Taipoksee! I wonder how he works his gravel!'

'I wonder, indeed!'

And when we saw him working it, we wondered still more.

At a quarter to eight next morning,—which, by the way, was February 19,—the first meal of the day being over, the Indians of Taipoksee's village, to our unmitigated astonishment, began clearing up and stowing away things generally. We thought they were about to start on some expedition. We were mistaken.

At eight o'clock the old chief Taipoksee came out of the doorway of his wigwam, and stood alone in the sun.

Like all the Choomteyas, he was above the middle height, almost black in colour, straight as an arrow, and —he was quite clean. An unexpected ending for the sentence, perhaps, and not very complimentary, but to those acquainted with Indian habits it will convey a pleasing fact ;—for, like all his people, he began each day with a plunge in the neighbouring stream. Alone, then, in the full blaze of the sunlight, stood the great chief of the Wakalla.

In the centre of the village was a huge redwood tree, and for a few minutes Taipoksee watched the shadow of its topmost branch, as it slowly glided over the ground. His right hand grasped a spear, his left hand rested on his hip. Suddenly he raised his hand from his hip and pointed to the sun, and in a voice of thunder he roared forth,—

' To work ! To work ! To work ! '

From all the wigwams of the village the men, women, and children came out, and marched steadily to the river bank just below the fall. The old men, the women, and the children carried the bowls and baskets and boards, such as were then used on the alluvial diggings. They were evidently going to work the gravel. But how ?

Taipoksee, still alone at the door of his wigwam, again roared forth,—

'To work! To work! To work!'

And, as we afterwards found, every one of his people not incapacitated by illness was forced to obey his command.

'To work! To work! To work!' shouted the chief for the last time. And the old men and the women and children stood ready for the gold-bearing soil, and the young and vigorous men had ranged themselves by the side of the stream.

Suddenly the man nearest to us stepped back a pace or two, gave a short run, and took a header into the pool below the fall. Another, and another, man after man, all along the line, went plunging in like porpoise after porpoise in a shoal. Soon the first man came to the surface, and trod water to the shore, where one of the squaws stood ready with a basin, into which he cast a handful of gravel.

As did the first, so did the rest. Each brought a handful from the bed of the pool, and threw it into the bowl that was held out for it. Then the men scrambled ashore. Rested for a minute or so, they took up their line again, and, man after man, in the same order as before, dived into the stream.

'What think you of the gold divers of the Wakalla?' asked Taipoksee, as he approached us.

'Is that the only way you get the gold?'

'The only way. The only gold there is is at the bottom of that pool, and there the gravel is as thick as the shade of the redwood tree!'

'Where does it come from?   .

'It comes from the hills of snow, from the home of the Awahnees.'

CHAPTER IV.

THE HOME OF THE AWAHNEES.

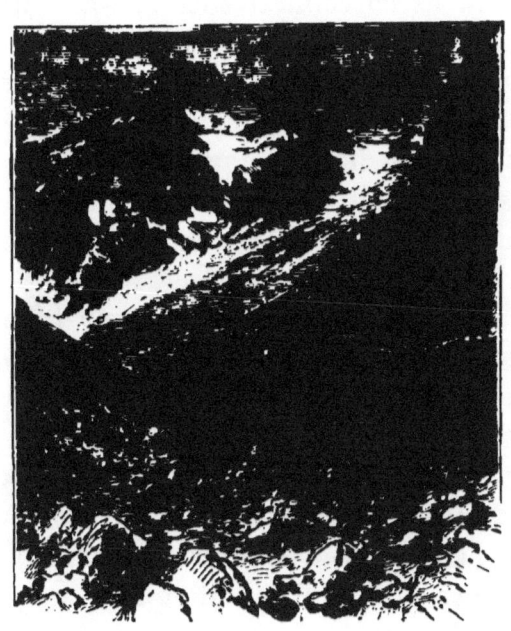

For a time we stood and watched the gold divers, and talked to Taipoksee of the difficulty he must have had in disciplining his people. Never before had I conceived it possible that an Indian settlement could be ruled like a factory village on the Atlantic coast. It was an ideal community. Every man, woman, and child was employed in a task for which they were most suited, and the ablest man, the only man amongst them who was fit for anything besides picking and diving, was in supreme command. Taipoksee's word was law. There was no question about that.

'Do your men always obey orders as they did this morning?' asked Ned.

'If one of my people disobeys me—he goes!'

'Goes where?'

'I do not care. He does not stay here alive!'

What has now become of the Choomteyas I know not. When we were amongst them they seemed a happy people, thriving exceedingly under their benevolent despotism. Taipoksee's character was quite a study; the combination of the Indian chief with the captain of industry and trader-in-general was to us so comical that it was with difficulty we could keep ourselves from laughing. In fact, on several occasions I did begin to laugh, but fortunately managed to ease off the outburst into an approving grin. The last time I did so, however, I noticed Taipoksee give me a sly, suspicious look, and I thought it best for the future to laugh with him and not at him.

He took us round the gold pans much as any other manager would do round his works. He explained how the gravel was washed and the gold secured, and how every month he sent off an instalment by his messengers, who returned with its value in dollars. He even showed us all the little contrivances by which he kept a check on his men's proceedings; and he seemed as pleased while he described them as a down-east Yankee telling how he got inside a patent. I took quite a fancy to the ingenious old tyrant, the first of his race I came across who was doing his best to swim with the civilizing stream. When he informed us in broken English that his working hours

were from eight to three, Ned's hilarity could no longer
be restrained.   He laughed loud and long.   Luckily
Taipoksee mistook the laugh for a compliment.

'First they would work only five hours; but I said
that was not enough, I must have six.   Then I said I
must have seven.   That is all I can get; but it is
enough.   "If you want eight hours," one squaw said,
"you must pay overtime."   "Overtime!" I said.   "Your
husband will no more go messages for me; he learns too
much!"   But I think it best to say no more about
eight hours!'

And the old fellow gave us a wink that would have
done credit to an Irishman.   I have always understood
he was a pure-blood Indian; but I have had my doubts.
That wink was a staggerer.

As soon as we civilly could, we bade adieu to the go-
ahead Choomteya, and started in chase of the Awahnees.
Taipoksee's advice was for us to cross the Wakalla, strike
north-east for a 'tree cave,' and then keep to the south-
east until we regained the river.   According to him the
river was no longer branchless; we were now on the
higher ground, and the feeders began to pour in from the
snow-fields in the distance.   Our road, we were warned,
would be a rough one; we would have to make our way
over hills and plains, by torrents and precipices, and
through marshes and forests; but the track was clear
enough, and afforded us a definite turning-point.   We
were also assured that game would be plentiful on the
march, and that we should in the end be able to approach
the Awahnees unobserved owing to their always using
the southerly route.   The only risky part of the road
seemed to curve through a patch of forest.

'But easy enough there,' said Taipoksee; 'him marked with skunk.'

'With skunk !' exclaimed both of us.

'It is so,' said Taipoksee, resuming the grand manner of the redskin warrior. 'You will smell your way through the forest, for the trail is marked with the bodies of the skunk in the manner of the Meewocs.'

'Do we follow that scent, or do we run away from it ?' asked I.

'I think we'd better go south,' said Reid. However, it appeared that the skunk novelty only extended through this forest, and, as we could easily keep 'just within range,' as Ned said, we resolved to start on the north side.

As the old chief had assumed his stilts, we bade him farewell in equally stilted phrase. In a few minutes we had taken our last look at the gold divers of the Wakalla. We were crossing the limestone range which was soon to lead us on to the mass of granite that forms the core of the Sierra. Far to the eastward we could see peak after peak fading away in the blue until they seemed in their gleaming whiteness to be but phantoms—the spirits of the hills in the age of ice. As an almost transparent speck we could see the tiny cloud that wreathes the bright gorget of the king of the Sierra, that granite helm with its plume of snow which crowns the summit of the highest mountain in North America.

And the plant-life wás changing as we rose higher towards our goal. The pale blue digger pine and black oak had been left behind; we were nearly through the zone of the redwood trees, and were soon to make our way among the pitches, and the sturdy sugars that boast the bunches of gigantic cones.

Keeping well to the north as soon as we struck the first feeder of the Wakalla, we trudged along steadily and cheerily to the tree cave. Our course was clear enough, albeit a rough one, and the only point where Ned found it necessary to pull up and reconnoitre was at the strip of the woodland which we soon discovered to have the trail through it marked with the skunks as hinted by Taipoksee. Fortunately the characteristic odour of these pests of the wilderness had been much modified by time. Here they were, hung up on the trees, one body just out of nose range of the other, so that, as Ned said 'the road was as clear as may be, if you'll only trust to common scents.' Keeping 'just within range' of the chaste perfume of the decaying carcass of the skunk, we found our way through the forest, and without adventure reached the tree cave at sundown the day after we left the Indian village.

This tree cave was just the place for a startling experience, and I often think that somehow or other we were either too soon or too late in getting there. With such surroundings we ought to have had a thrilling adventure ; but all that happened was a snowstorm which kept us prisoners for a day. It was merely an ordinary fall of the blinding sort ; but, from what the Choomteya had told us, we felt sure of closing with the Awahnees, and, as the horses were safe, a day more or less mattered but little. The cave was a wide crack in the limestone some hundred and forty by ninety feet in area, running off into smaller cavities around. In its floor was a pool that seemed over thirty feet deep ; the top was open to the sky, and from the overhanging cliff to the water was at least six-and-thirty yards. The strangest part about the cave, was the magnificent maple tree which rose from within, and towered upwards many feet above the rift, looking like a dwarf on the hill side.

We were very comfortable in the cave; we had been fortunate in keeping the larder well supplied, and we spent the time contentedly enough discussing the chances of our success on the three matters in which we were interested. I need not dwell on what was said; the result was very fairly summarised by Reid as he was making himself straight for the night.

'Number one is Zeke—verdict, we shall see him. Number two is your gravel pit — verdict, doubtful. Number three is your craze about the Barber—verdict, very doubtful. Who is that fellow? He was not an Awahnee, he was not a Choomteya, he was not a plains Digger; and all of them differ in their marks and build. Who are all these fellows, if it comes to that? Seems to be rather mixed, anyhow. Good-night!'

The next morning the snow had ceased and mostly gone. We were early afoot and away. At first we kept south-east as we had been advised, but after a time we found the road getting difficult, and unfortunately bore more and more to the south, so as to strike the main river. A foolish thing this proved to be. All that day neither of us got a shot, and very glum were we when we took up our quarters for the night among a mass of rock at the head of one of the lesser canyons. The night was cold, and at daybreak we started, hoping for better luck and a better road. We had neither; and it is now a wonder to me how we got on as we did. Reid wished to follow up one of the canyons, and take a parallel course some dozen miles to the northward. This would have been by far the best plan. But somehow I felt that we were doing right in sticking to the route we had chosen, and, instead of my accompanying Ned, Ned gave in to me. As events proved, my obstinacy was justified, or rather excused. We certainly arrived at the nick of time, and we could have done no good had we reached our goal a day or two earlier.

There is a great satisfaction in reasoning yourself out to be right when your stomach tells you you are wrong, and this I felt acutely during that cold wearying day up and down the rocks and gullies that fringe the Wakalla. From early morning we had been at the same work, and not a sign of animal life had we seen. Our provisions were running short, and we had placed ourselves on half allowance, so that it was with the gloomiest forebodings that hour after hour went by, and no game hove in sight to cheer our painful advance.

At last, when well on in the afternoon, as we were crossing a strip of tableland between two strings of precipices, I happened to look away to windward, and just beyond the nearest ridge I caught sight of a herd of strange animals, three-quarters sheep and one quarter deer. They were about a mile off, and were slowly moving towards us, grazing as they came.

'Bighorn!' said Ned; 'I never knew they ranged this side of the Sierra. Stoop down behind that bush, keep still as a mouse, and let them saunter on.' And stretched at full length, with our rifles laid so as to be ready when the heads rose into view, we crouched there and waited. The bighorn did 'saunter' most cruelly. We must have remained silent and motionless for quite an hour. Cramped with the long stay in the one position, I was

'UNCEASINGLY RAGED THE BOOM AND ROAR.'

just drawing up my legs to rise when Ned touched me. There, through the bush, about a cricket pitch in front of us, I saw the finest head and horns it has ever been my lot to meet with. The ram stood boldly facing us, gazing full at the shrub which formed our cover. Long and thoughtfully he peered into it, until he was joined by his companions, who all favoured us with a stare. Theirs was but an indifferent gaze, however; his seemed to pierce the foliage and contemplate the danger he knew not how to avoid. I was bending to fire when Ned whispered me to wait. And immediately, as if by magic, the heads had disappeared. The herd, about a score in number, had turned sharp round and noiselessly stolen away.

Night was closing in, and all we could do was to camp near by and follow the trail in the morning. Close to us one of the ravines ran deep into the plateau; stealthily we crept to it, and down among the rocks we huddled together, in a sort of shallow cave, and, with as little noise as possible, made ourselves comfortable for the night. I say made ourselves comfortable, but most of the comfort consisted in anticipation; for, truth to tell, we felt much as a gambler is supposed to feel when he makes his last throw. Our last piece of deer flesh formed our supper, and, as there was a possibility of the pair of horns rising in front of us at any moment, we ate it as if we were afraid that our jaws would creak and betray our whereabouts. Wearied out, I fell asleep and dreamt the day's journey over again. Again I saw the bighorn, again he came and looked at me, again I grasped my rifle to fire. There, between us and the stars, stood the gigantic head, deliberately moving towards me. I stretched out my hand, and was tugged into consciousness by a grip from

Reid, who said he thought it was about time for him to sleep. And sleep he did, according to his account, 'without any such silly fancies.'

At daybreak we crept away in search of the ram. A sprinkling of snow had fallen during the night, and among the higher rocks we soon came upon his tracks. Evidently the whole herd had passed along the ledge we were following. Bare and rugged were the rocks of the ravine, and wilder grew the gap as we tracked the bighorn among the crags. Soon the ledge narrowed, and Ned proposed that one alone should go on.

'No,' said I; 'let us both go, and one can help the other.'

I went first. I was the lightest, and the most sanguine. The spoor was sharp and undisturbed, and among the many footprints we could easily identify those of our thoughtful patriarch. It was cold work creeping along the shelf which led round the face of a canyon, and up into a narrow branch where a recent slip had broken back into the wall. For half an hour we followed the foot-prints. At times the ledge was so narrow that we had to stand upright with our backs to the rock that towered above us.

We shuffled along sideways like ghosts at a play. A hundred yards below us leapt the torrent; a hundred feet above us rose the grey wall; to the right and left stretched the white ribbon of snow, dotted with the spoor of the bighorn. Often the brink of the precipice was only an inch or two from our toes as we sidled round the critical points. Once or twice the look-down was so terrible, that my head grew light, and it was with difficulty I could force myself back against the wall. A frightful propensity developed itself within me ; it seemed as though I must lean forward and strive to float on the air of the canyon. When we came to where the ledge widened, I

turned my face to the wall, and along the first and second narrows after I passed safely ; but at the third narrowing it seemed as though I must push myself backwards. I kept my hands flat against the rock; but, in spite of myself, the muscles would contract, they would attempt to spring me over. I thought I was lost; move I could not; I was going, when I caught sight of the spoor of the bighorn extending on each side of me, and my reason told me that where there was room for a sheep to walk there was room for a man to stand. The thought gave me back my ballast, and I crept away again. Reid was cooler, but, as he afterwards confessed, 'felt a bit skeery.' He knew that where the bighorn went he could go, 'provided they walked;' and he followed me round the cliff, but he dared not speak for fear of giving an alarm.

Thus did we advance in mid-air; and in the end we found that the bighorn had leapt a chasm some four feet broad, and continued their journey back and round the opposite ledge. With that awful depth frowning beneath me, I dared not follow. I could hardly step; to jump was impossible. The 'taking off' was not more than twenty inches, the landing was hardly as wide; between was a gash three hundred feet straight down. Mad though we were at our want of faith in our surefootedness, we agreed that 'it was hardly worth while,' and began the return journey. When we came we had all the excitement of hope to lead us on; as we went back we had nothing but despair. Judge then of my thoughts and fears as we made the perilous journey the second time.

But we did not give up the bighorn. Reid was decided as to that. To him the voyage along the ledge was a 'curious experience,' all in the day's march. He had made up his mind to have a bighorn steak for breakfast; he had convinced himself it was his duty to get that steak; and through fire and water he would unflinchingly go until that steak was got. So we went down and round for a mile or more, and at a lower level found the track. We made another skirt of the precipice. Ned went first.

'Excuse me, sir,' said he, with a grin, 'you've had your chance. Turn about, you know, and my turn now.' Again we had at times to creep and at times to sidle, but the road proved unbroken. To Ned's gratification, 'the beggars walked; none of their skylarking jumps.' And eventually we sighted the ram and his family.

Reid motioned to me to take the ram, while he aimed at a yearling. I thought this was considerate of him; so it was, but in a different sense to what I imagined. We fired, and both hit. The ram fell dead, with his backbone smashed; the yearling gave a wonderful writhing skip, and toppled over, shot through the brain. The rest of the herd fled like the wind.

'Glad I didn't miss,' said Ned. 'Your ram is a good one to look at, but the youngster will give us the best breakfast.'

The breakfast was a long time coming, for we had again to retreat, and make a considerable circuit before we found our game. The yearling was soon disposed of to advantage. The horns of the ram were immense; they measured eighteen inches in circumference at the base. They were the largest Ned or I had heard of, and the largest but two that I have since read about.

Our chase of the bighorn led us into better ground. Our difficulties for a time were over. We started straight away across a long rolling slope, gradually ascending as we went. We camped for the night as cheerfully as we had done in the tree cave, and in the morning resumed our journey to the east. We expected to get within sight of the Indian camp before sundown.

We had now passed beyond the zone of the pitch and sugar pines, and were among the firs and tamaracks.

Every now and then we passed through strips of forest, and as we crossed the rising ground we could see the trees gradually thin off in the distance, as they straggled up the sides of the snow-clad hills. About noon we passed a long open strip from which the trees in front seemed to extend right away for several miles. As we sat and rested, we could hear the murmur of falling waters borne towards us by the southerly wind.

'A waterfall on the Wakalla,' said Reid.

'Yes, let us make for it; we cannot be far wrong now.'

The apparently wide patch of forest barred the way. As we were in the enemy's country, we advanced with all due caution. We expected at least a five-mile walk before we reached the river. The forest was a mere strip; we were soon through it, and out on the flat. And in a few minutes there swiftly unrolled itself before us the most astonishing scene that ever greeted the eyes of man.

We were on the brink of a narrow valley half a mile wide and three or four miles long. The walls of the valley were cruel, bare, grey granite, with here and there a stripe of black or brown; and these walls were vertical. It seemed as though a knot in the plain had been cut round like a piece of a puzzle and slipped bodily towards the centre of the earth. It had slipped so deep that at first our eyes refused to grasp the magnitude of the cataclysm. Those vertical scarps of rock rose nearly three thousand feet from the ground. The cross of St. Paul's Cathedral is three hundred and sixty feet from the churchyard pavement; figure to yourselves eight such cathedrals piled one on top of the other, and you have the height of the Awahnee valley.

And over these astonishing walls poured the waters from the higher country. Around us the winter had nearly gone; beyond us we could see the snows still low on the mountain sides; beneath us was a different climate altogether. The upper lands were in mid-winter, the valley was in early spring. From the melting snows the 'streams were almost choked with water, and down they came steadily along the high plateau, to leap wildly and determinedly into the river, which, like a glittering tape, lay seemingly motionless beneath.

Over a hundred cataracts did we count as they broke into foam at the foot of the cliffs,—some roaring down in one straight stream, others shattered again and again on projecting ledges before they vanished behind the pigmy trees that fringed the granite scarp. Here was a group of ten; here, a group of six; there, nine narrow streaks marked out the wall at regular intervals. To the right, to the left, all around us, the water went pouring in; the heavy falls sternly, strongly, and steadily drenching down; the lighter falls swaying in the breeze, feathering and breaking into spray, and ever sprinkling off new showers of crystal to sparkle like brilliants in the glorious sun. The arch of the rainbow rose from many a rippling cloud, and in one of the nooks we could see the circle complete. We were afterwards to learn of another, where three full rings are shown, how its spirit breathed on three Indian girls and bewitched them, so that their spirits still dwell among the falling waters.

We gazed for a time in awe. Not a word of gratification or surprise escaped our lips. We looked at the cliffs, and we looked at the waterfalls, and we looked at the trees, and we looked at the central stream. And it was not until we had looked at them and thought of them again and again that our tiring eyes began to wander. I say 'our,' but I think I could have stood there at gaze till the evening. It was Ned who broke the spell.

'Look! look! Those buttons are wigwams, and those ants are horses.'

CHAPTER V.

THE GRIZZLY INTERVENES.

THE village lay amid a few trees on the bank of the middle stream. In the narrow straggling meadows we could see the horses leisurely grazing. From the height at which we were above them they were about the size of rice grains, and the wigwams, as Ned said, were no bigger than buttons.

'Keep back; the Awahnees may see us.'

'Not they,' answered Reid. 'They are in another world down there. Luckily for us, we missed the road. Their look-out is down the western throat of the valley and up the slopes that guard its flanks. They never expect an attack from the upper country. However, we may as well have a rest.'

And he flung himself full length on the ground by the side of one of the torrents, and watched its waters as they fell over the precipice. I joined him, and for some minutes we remained speechless. I was off into dreamland, half hushed to sleep by the silvery music of the cascades.

'Wonder,' said Ned at last,—'wonder which of these falls your gravel comes down?'

'Oh! ah!' said I. 'I had forgotten all about that. Which should you think?'

'Well, perhaps the whole hundred of them.'

'Then I'm afraid your share isn't worth much.'

'Nor yours. But cheer up. If "the farther you go the more you get" holds good, the central stream ought to be the richest. It comes from the high level, and yet has got down there. It looks to me as though it flowed into the valley as a river, not as a cascade. If so, we had better strike it higher up. We can then work down to those fellows from the unguarded-side, and make our observations.'

'What are we to do then?'

'Keep quiet, find out all we can, wait for M'Quarrie's people, and when they come claim the valley as first finders. It would make a nice little farm.'

'Very. But how about the present owners?'

'They turned out those that were here before them, and out they'll go before their betters. It is the same old game ever since the world began; if you can't keep a thing, you must drop it. All men have to do it whether they like it or not. All the beasts have done it. And even those firs could only have got a footing there by crowding out some other green thing.'

'Then the strongest always win ?'

'Yes, but only when they are the cleverest. Fact is, you are not strong unless you have got thinking strength and downright genuine justice behind you !'

'Which, of course, you have ?'

'We should never do anything in this world if we didn't believe we had.'

'I believe in good, honest, steady work.'

'Seems so, doesn't it ?' said Ned, with a twinkle in his eye. 'Nothing like pegging away, sailoring, for instance ?'

The question was a poser.

'You see there is a difference between preaching and practising,' I remarked ; feebly, I admit.

'There is indeed,' said Ned ; 'but, as the preaching is only a means to the practising, you are judged by the practising.'

'Now be candid, Ned ; you don't want to steal all that belongs to the Indians ?'

'No, not all ; let us only steal the bit that has got the gravel. Honestly and steadily work it, eh ? And buy up the rest of the valley with the profit from the stolen patch. That is the usual trade, isn't it ? Takings are keepings in another form, you see. It sounds cruel, and we ought to stop it, but how ?'

'You are a philosopher, Ned, and of the old shocking school. How about your horse, for instance ; are takings to be keepings there ?'

'Not if I can help it. And we shan't turn the Diggers out—if they can help it. But out they'll go, as safe as eggs ; for this valley of theirs is too good for the likes of them !'

'And how about the Barber ?'

'Oh, bother the Barber! If he's here he'll turn up
safe enough. I shouldn't wonder if he isn't the chief or
the opposition boss of the Awahnees.'

'But you said he wasn't an Awahnee!'

'No more I think he is, now you remind me. But
come on; we must keep our eyes open. Those fellows
down there are too comfortable to run far. Let us get
along to the east, and see if there is any way into this
Digger trap. It is a curious place; so was Death Valley.
Who would have thought that our earth had such holes
in it!'

Following the run of the marvellous valley, we made
our way to the east. We had to cross many streams, all
of which were pouring their waters over the cliffs. The
scenery was magnificent. Never before, or since, did I
see such a land. Every few yards fresh beauties opened
upon us. I gazed wonder-struck. Ned took it all very
coolly, remarked that the snow was still hanging about,
supposed that we should have a bad time of it if we did
not get down soon, guessed that Caffrey would take the
south trail and come in on the other side, etc. etc. At
last I grew quite angry with him.

'Why don't you wake up, Ned, and drop your selfish-
ness? Look round you and enjoy the finest sight your
eyes ever looked on.'

'I do enjoy the sight, and I am not so selfish as you
take me for. But I see bows and arrows as well as waterfalls, and I am not easy in my mind.'

'Well, we shall be in for it if we stop. Shall we go
back?'

'No. I mean to stay. But, as far as I can see, we can
do nothing. Do you know, I feel as if I was being

bewitched, or electrified, or something of that sort. That water streaking down seems to be charming something out of me or into me. And now the clouds have begun to drift across the sun, I seem to be troubled as the shadows run along these cliffs. Fact! I feel as I did when I looked into that waggon. And I don't like it!'

The conversation dropped as we crossed a torrent that seemed to go roaring by with glee at the glorious jump in front of it. Reid was right as to the central stream. The Wakalla flowed in as a river; it did not leap in as a cataract. It divided the valley; the rift was but an expansion of its canyon.

For five or six miles we kept on before we found a practicable descent. The farther we went the higher we got, and soon we reached the snow line. Just on the border we sighted a herd of wapiti, some feeding on the miserable grass, others couching dreamily on the snow. There were about twenty of them in all, and, after an exciting stalk, which I need not stop to describe, we bagged four. The pursuit led us down almost to the bank of the Wakalla. Fortunately the bulls fell near together.

When we had dropped the last we looked round for a camping-place, as, though it was early, the abundance of food thus suddenly fallen to us was worth securing. Near us, at the foot of a precipice, was a heap of fragmentary granite, brought down by a recent fall, which had marked a long scar on the face of the cliff. The masses had piled themselves up as though to form a Cyclopean temple. Huge stones, as big as the sarsens of Stonehenge, lay tumbled on and against each other like nursery bricks ; and just as bricks often fall when thrown away in confusion, so had these rugged monoliths.

Facing us was a fairly good doorway. The lintel was certainly not straight, but still it was there. Entering the doorway, we found ourselves in a somewhat angular space entirely enclosed on the sides and top. From it a narrow passage between two upright blocks led to another and larger wedge-like area, which was open to the sky only by a narrow crack about a yard long and five or six inches wide. In all directions openings led off between the stones; some shut suddenly off by a sharp angle, others leading farther than we then cared to look.

We passed through the doorway. All seemed quiet and safe. We explored the first chamber, which was only just high enough to allow of Reid standing upright. It aroused no suspicion. We then entered the second chamber, which was about a yard higher, say, nine feet in all, for Ned was as nearly as possible six feet, straight and sinewy as one of Cooper's backwoodsmen. The second chamber was all clear, and the cracks and cavities, being peered into, seemed to be all void and new.

'Just the place for a comfortable camp!' said Reid; 'and within easy range of our coloured friends. There's the river, which we can prospect for its gravel, and that tiny stream running through the hole in the back room we can use for drinking. By-the-bye,' and Ned went out and looked up at the cliff, 'that stream would be better if it didn't come down just there; that ravine is a little too full of snow to please me. But I suppose the water will carry it off.'

'Oh, there's no fear from that!' said I; 'we can't better this. We are well sheltered by the cliff, and if the founder has only just occurred, as, judging from all these fresh edges of rock, it seems reasonable to suppose, why,

E

we are the first comers, and the Diggers have never been here.'

'Hum!' said Ned; 'let us just take a look around.'

And a 'look around' we took, and all seemed satis-factory. So, with much effort, we got our four deer into the second chamber. And when we had done this, which was by no means an easy task, for we had to bring one of the bulls quite a quarter of a mile, we set to work to have a good meal and make ourselves generally comfortable.

The sun set, and, as the fading daylight died away, the moon grew bright. From a milky disc on a curtain of grey we watched her grow to a gleaming sphere on a canopy of violet blue. The stars came out to gem the heavens, but their light was lost in the silver radiance of the queen of the night. We could hear the ripple of the streams near at hand, and we could hear the murmured music of the falls in the valley, as it was fitfully borne by us on the breeze. Suddenly there was a distant noise, as of something fallen from a height.

' What's that ? ' said I.

' Let us go and see,' said Ned. 'I feel as though some-thing was giving us the slip. Let us be off by moonlight down the valley.'

' Agreed,' said I; 'but what a fellow you are for feelings and fancies! You are as bad as an Æolian harp, and sound to every puff that comes.'

'Well, I can't go far wrong if the puff comes from the right quarter.'

Down the valley we went, and nothing did we see of the cause of the fall ; but we saw many other things that we did not go to look for, and which made that moonlight walk the most memorable expedition of my life. It was

as light as day, but the shadows were deeper, and the
light had that strange effulgence which only the moonrays
give. From our doorway the view down the river was
fine enough, but, when we turned the buttress that barred
the way, and could look some distance before us, it seemed
as though we were gazing into fairyland. Immediately
in front was a magic mirror, the slightly rippled surface
of a lake through which the stream flowed. On either
side the rocks rose high, and their summits stretched up
to the very stars. Soon we were in the valley itself. As
it widened, the waterfalls were gradually revealed; and,
after crossing the innumerable tributaries of the main
stream, we at last reached the centre, and took a long
look round us. What the scene was from the top during
the daylight I have done my best to tell; what it was
from below, in the moonlight, I must leave to your
imagination.

Where the valley was widest its width could not be
more than eight hundred yards, and of this about five-and-
twenty were taken up by the Wakalla, which, flowing first
on one side and then on the other, alternately touched the
fallen fragments at the foot of the cliffs. By the river
side were alders, and willows, and Gilead balm, and
patches of bush and underwood, raspberries, pentstemons,
ferns, and wild roses. On the low granite heaps were
oaks and maples and laurels. Behind them was the grey
wall of rock, hidden every now and then by the curtain of
falling water glittering in the light of the moon. In
places the granite wall was broken back ; and in places it
was buttressed by square-cut massive towers, one of which,
three thousand three hundred feet high, can be seen from
the San Joaquin, sixty miles away as the crow flies. And

on both sides the wall was the same, the dark fringe of
the trees, the ashen rock, and the crystal veils with their
upper curves like silver bars, and their edges and folds of
mist and cloud; and unceasingly raged the boom and
roar of the cascades, and the seethe and hiss of the rapids
and streams.

As we neared the village we could see the lights moving
about, and we heard a sound as of revelry. Cautiously
approaching under cover of the bushes, we found that a
great festival was in progress, and a ceremonial dance was
in full swing. As the well-built, athletic figures of the
Awahnees moved round the fire in the moonlight,
advancing and retiring, sidling and wriggling, writhing
and leaping, the thought struck me that they looked much
as elves would look if seen through a microscope. What
Ned compared them to may be imagined; but his criti-
cism was prejudiced. We watched them and waited.
At last the dance ended, and the dancers, now joined by
the women, moved towards us, and, circling round what
looked like a huge cradle, indulged in a grand finale of
the most astonishing yells and gestures. This they kept
up till they quite tired themselves out; and then, with a
farewell insult hurled at the cradle, each of the performers
went home.

The dance was over, and all was still. We waited
and watched for an hour in the solitude. No one stirred
in the Indian camp. All seemed asleep.

'What is that cradle?' I whispered to Reid.

'Can't make out. Is it worth having a look?'

'Yes; but are we safe?'

'I think so. They are all done up.'

Stealthily we moved nearer in the shadow. From tree

to tree we crept, and in a few minutes reached the cradle. It was a rough framework of twigs, plaited in and out like a hurdle and shaped like a dome. Beneath it was a pair of saplings crossed, and to these saplings there was tied a man who lay fast asleep. The moon shone full on the cradle, and the light streamed in through the gaps on to the face of the sleeper.

'By all that's wonderful,' hissed Reid under his breath, 'it's the Barber!'

And so it was.

'He's a prisoner,' said Ned; 'and they'll murder him or burn him at sunrise.'

'Not if I know it,' said I.

'Whisht! Get under cover again, and watch.'

For a quarter of an hour we remained silent. Nothing stirred in the camp.

'Now,' said Ned, 'you keep guard, and I'll cut those twigs off pretty sharp. Are your revolvers loaded?'

'Yes.'

'Then don't fire if you can help it. If anything goes wrong, run for our rubbish heap.'

Ned stepped up to the cradle. Swiftly the knife flashed in the moonlight. Silently he lifted the cage, and then, with a touch to the Digger to wake him, he severed the bands at his hands and feet.

The Indian was free!

With a bound he was at my side, and all seemed over, when from the nearest wigwam a gigantic Awahnee rushed to the cage, and, seeing it empty, turned round to look. As he dashed up to the cage we three scuttled off. With a yell that woke the village he was after us. On we went, making the best of our start, out into the open straight for the head of the valley, the Awahnee after us, and all the warriors of the tribe bounding after him in a straggling line.

'Run for your lives!' said Ned.

And run we did ; but we did not gain on the pursuers.

When we reached the narrowing of the valley, it became evident that we would have to fight. The Barber was tiring, and would have to be left behind if our safety was to depend on our running powers. The Awahnee was gradually gaining ; and the yelling tribe behind showed no sign of giving out either in voice or speed.

In front of us was a fallen tree, and the only passage was round it or over it. Ned led the way round its roots. I was hardly a yard behind. As we placed the tree between us and our pursuers, Ned called me to halt,

and we swung round to defend ourselves. The Barber followed, the leading Awahnec not ten feet behind him.

As I raised my rifle I saw something move at the roots of the tree. A grey mass rose full in the moonlight. With a yell the Barber leapt over it. But the Awahnee saw it not till he rounded ; and before he could leap, or save, or defend himself, he was clasped in the relentless hug of a furious grizzly bear.

CHAPTER VI.

THE LOST KAREYA.

 The pursuers halted in dismay. As the stragglers closed up confusedly, there rose from the excited crowd a wild shout of terror.

'Uzumaitee! Uzumaitee! The grizzly bear! The grizzly bear!'

The man was to be left to fight out the battle alone !

The moon had now risen to its height in the heavens ; and in the full wealth of its brilliant rays every detail of the duel could be watched. Across the path lay the tree, its topmost boughs dipped in the Wakalla, its wide-spreading roots torn up from the mound at the base of the precipice and stretched forth like the scraggy limbs of a school of hags, to leave a gap some six feet in width between them and the wall.

In the gap the struggle took place. It raged in duplicate. There bent and swayed the writhing group of the strugglers ; and there bent and swayed in unison the group's dark short shadow cast by the light of the moon. The sharp, unblurred phantom seemed as real as the substance. The death wrestle did not last long. The man fought his utmost in vain. Soon he dealt the bear a mortal wound, and the pain drove the brute to frenzy. Crushing the life out of the Awahnee, it bore him to the ground. The shadows parted. Rushing at the cowering crowd behind, the grizzly scattered them as if they were all in shadow-land. And then it stumbled, and snarled, and stopped, rolled over, kicked, and died.

But while the fight was on we had continued our retreat, looking back every few moments to watch its progress; and we saw it end from the higher ground. Then we ran again by the river bank, and then in the shade of the trees, and then out again into the moon-light, until we reached our stronghold. The Indians resumed the chase as soon as the bear died, but we had gained considerably on them, and our plunge into the shadow put them off the trail. The trail they soon took up; and about a quarter of an hour after we reached our temple, or cave, or rubbish heap, or whatever it should be called, we saw the leaders appear round the left buttress that shut out our view down the valley.

Meanwhile we had not been idle. In front of the doorway were a few smaller lumps of granite, which we piled up as a breastwork; for further retreat was not to be thought of, and our only hope of safety lay in standing a siege until M'Quarrie's men found their way to the village.

As soon as he entered the cave, Ned ran to see if the deer were safe.

'All right!' he said cheerily; 'we have got enough grub to last us for a week or two, if the Digger don't make a beast of himself.'

I saw the Barber give him a look straight in the face. Their eyes met. It was only for an instant, but it was enough.

Reid held out his hand.

'Give us a grip to show there's no ill-feeling. You didn't steal those horses?'

'No. They stole me.'

'What! the horses?' said Ned, with a smirk, 'or those cowardly skunks?'

'The Awahnees.'

'Are you one of them?'

'No.'

'Were you ever one of them?'

'No.'

'Then who— All right! we are all together. Just give us a hand with these stones outside; and, Langham, have the barkers ready. This is an awkward job, but at least we have done the right thing in saving a man from being roasted.'

And so we piled up the blocks in the doorway. And we had only just placed the four on the top, leaving three narrow gaps between them, when, as I have said, the leader of the Awahnees appeared round the buttress.

It was not until I learned that he was destined to be head torturer in the ceremony of the morning that I ceased to regret his fate.

'Better begin as we intend to go on,' said Ned. 'If the grizzly takes number one, and I take number two, those thieving brutes may knock under.'

And as deliberately as Ned covered the bighorn, so did he cover the Awahnee. And just as the bighorn died without a groan, so did the Indian.

'Better lend the Barber your spare revolver,' said Reid as he reloaded.

There was no immediate occasion to use it.

The death of the first in the chase had its influence. The Awahnees drew back. For a few minutes we saw and heard nothing but the flow of the river and the quiver of the boughs as the wind sighed through them laden with the chorus of the distant cascades.

Then the branch of a tree was waved up and down the edge of the rock.

'Flag of truce,' said I.

'Looks like it,' said Reid. 'I wish they'd wait till daylight, though. I don't like this moonlight business.'

From the rock into the open there stepped an Indian, with his bow slung over his shoulder and the branch in his hand. In answer I waved my handkerchief; and, alone, he came towards us.

'Shall we go out to meet him?' said I.

'No,' said Reid. 'Let him come within hailing distance and shout what he has got to say.'

'But that's not civilized warfare!'

'Who said it was? Is any of it civilized warfare? Is it civilized warfare to steal a man's horses? Is it civilized warfare to kidnap a poor beggar, and keep him for days, till the moon or the sun happens to rise over a particular raspberry bush, before you roast him or boil him? Is it civilized warfare to tie a poor fellow wrist and ankle to a pair of trees, and dance round him till your throat goes dry with the hot insults you have shovelled out on to him? No, it isn't! Let the beggar come and shout.'

The 'beggar' did come, and he did 'shout.' He was an old, well-built fellow, of about the middle height,

whose low, broad shoulders and deep chest showed that
in early manhood he had been as athletic as his fellows.
Now, as generally happens, his broad shoulders had
developed and gained in fat, and he was somewhat
unwieldy. With great dignity he approached us, waving
the branch as he did so.

'That's the olive branch,' said I.

'No, it isn't,' said Ned; 'but it ought to be. It does
as well. A fat fellow like that might wave anything,
and we'd fancy he was a messenger of peace. I wonder
what the game is?'

The Awahnee came up fearlessly to within about fifteen
feet of our door. Then he stopped, waved his branch to
the right, to the left, to the ground, to the moon, and
then across his body.

'I am Awuyah,' he shouted, 'and I come from Tenaya,
the chief of the Awahnees!' And he paused.

'He wants you to say who we are,' said Ned. 'You'd
better answer.'

'What shall I tell him?'

'Oh, anything that sounds grand. Tell him a song,
but drawl it slowly. Say we are the hopefuls of George
Washington and William Shakespeare.'

'We are the potent signiors of the—of the—of the
what, Reid?'

'Of the Western Sea.'

'We are the potent signiors of the Western Sea. We come
to you with the power of the Langham and the Reid.'

'Tenaya welcomes the Langham and the Reid, and he
says that his thoughts are peace.'

'He's very kind,' said Ned. 'Give the old man an
echo. Tell him to drive on, or something.'

'Proceed, Awuyah!' said I, with dignity.

'Tenaya claims his prisoner, Owyanu, the outcast.'

'What prisoner?'

'Owyanu, the outcast from amongst men.'

'I am Owyanu,' said the Barber quietly.

'And the outcast from amongst men?' asked Reid, looking at him, or perhaps I ought to say looking through him.

'Awuyah says so.'

'Give him his echo,' said Ned. 'Ask him what next?'

'What further says Tenaya?'

'He says that he wants but Owyanu, his rightful captive according to all the laws of the Meewocs.'

'I am not a Meewoc,' said the Barber.

'And then?' said I to the herald.

'Tenaya desires to live at peace with the white men. He wants not their goods nor their horses. He will give you back the horses his people took from the San Joaquin, he will add to them ten horses of his own, if Owyanu, the outcast, is given up to suffer the penalty he has earned.'

'And what is that penalty?'

'To die the death of a traitor when the rays of the rising sun rest first upon Tisseyak.'

'Tell him,' said Reid, 'that the what-you-may-call-'ems of the Western Sea care not a dollar for Tisseyak, and that they know better than trust to the promises of a thieving Digger.'

'The horses,' continued Awuyah, 'will be brought to you, and Tenaya will guide you home.'

'To steal them again, I have no doubt,' said Reid.

' I don't think that,' said I.   ' They evidently want our friend.'

' What have you done, Mr. Barber?' asked Ned.

' It is a long story.'

' Have you murdered anybody?'   ' No.'

' Shot anybody?'   ' No.'

' Robbed anybody?'   ' No.'

' Damaged anybody?'   ' No.'

' Sold anybody?'   ' No.'

' Are you really the man Tenaya means?'   ' I am.'

' Used you to live here?'   ' No.'

' Were you ever in this valley before?'   ' No.'

' Then what have you got to do with Tenaya?'

' It is a long story.'

' Will they kill you if we give you up?'

' They will.'

' And they were keeping you for a show to-morrow, eh?'

' They were.'

' And you had no hand in stealing our horses?'

' None.'

' Then tell Awuyah,' said Reid to me, ' to tell Tenaya that we have found an honest man, and we will fight for him as long as we've limbs to defend ourselves.   Tell him his warriors will fall as they did before the grizzly and my number one.   But don't tell him that Caffrey's on the way, and quite able to take over the horses for himself.'

' Then you won't give up the Barber?'

' No; of course not.'

' We might get a grant of our gravel pit.'

' Eh? what?   Would you give up a man to torture for the sake of a gravel pit?'

' No; but from what you said, I thought you might.'

'Then you don't know Ned Reid. You should judge him by his practice, and not by his preaching. Tell that pompous Digger to clear off.'

In the nearest approach to blank verse that I could

manage, I shouted to Awuyah that Owyanu was our friend, and that we would defend him to the last.

'Tell him we can get out when we like,' said Ned.

The which I duly did.

Awuyah listened, courteous and unmoved.

'It is not true,' he said, 'that you can depart when
you please. There are but three of you, and the paths
are not known to you. The Awahnees are many and
brave, and though many may fall the victory will be
theirs. Tenaya wishes you well. Give up Owyanu. He
is the outcast of his tribe and his race, and the curse will
never depart from him. He can never prosper, nor can
he rest. Hunted from hill to hill, all that shelter
him will die. It is not our law ; it is the law of all that
dwell to the east and west of the mountains of snow.
Think what you are doing. Tenaya gives you grace ; he
will not attack you until the rays of the moon fall full on
the flank of Tutakanoola. I will come again.'

And with much dignity Awuyah withdrew.

'Now, what is all this mystery ?' said I to the Barber.
'Tell us what it means. Who are you ?'

'I am Owyanu, the lost Kareya.'

'And who, or what is that ?' asked Reid.

'I am not an Awahnee ; I am not a Meewoc. I am
a chief of the Kahrocs, the noblest of the tribes of the
Pacific slope. But, though there are many tribes, they
are but one people, and all combine to curse when one
begins. I came of a sacred family, and I grew up hoping
to be the chief of all my tribe. The Meewocs know no
future, and think of nothing but what they see ; but
the Kahrocs have other thoughts, and worship the great
Kareya. I was to be the priest of the great Kareya, and
the hour of my initiation drew nigh. I was to go to the
mountains to bring home the sacred fire which is fed by
the branches cut from the wondrous tree. The summit
of that tree grows in the shape of a man's head and
outstretched arms, and to trim it is to weep.'

'Never mind the fire; go on,' said Reid. 'We must have an answer ready for Awuyah. Tell us what you have done.'

'I was to go to the mountains to bring home the sacred fire; and I was to see the great Kareya, whose viceroy I was to be. I went forth with a companion, who was chosen for me, on what you call the 21st of last August. We went into the woods, and up into the mountains, and he told me I must fast. He could eat the porridge of the acorns, but I must not. We wandered many a mile up even into the snow, and looked forth to the eastern hills till we saw the sun rise from lower than I ever saw it before. Then we returned, and not far from our village, deep in the woods, we rested till it was time. Though my companion could eat, I must not; and with hunger I grew thin and feeble until I could hardly stand. Seeing me growing so weak, my companion gave me a little acorn porridge, but that was all. I asked him to teach me the knowledge of my people, but he said there was no knowledge. I asked him of the great Kareya, and he told me many strange legends, but nothing that I thought was true. All I asked was answered; but the answer was that in the future I should know. I asked if he intended to kill me when I grew too weak, but he showed me how all the others that were before me had gone through the same trial and had survived. For ten days were we away in the woods, I being supposed to learn all wisdom, and learning nothing but pain and foolishness. At last the time came for us to return. It was the 1st of September, the great day of the Kahroc year, when we approached the village. There all the people were gathered from far and near for the dance of

F

propitiation. My companion left me almost dying by the trees, and from the summit of the hill that overlooked our village shouted forth the news that the Kareya was coming. Then all the people fled in terror, for it was death for any to behold me. Some wrapped their heads in their blankets, some lay with their faces to the ground, some shut themselves up in their wigwams. For none must look upon the Kareya. As I was so weak and helpless, my companion summoned a guard to help me. Four there were of them, and, as they came up the hill to him, he descended to meet them, and blindfolded them one after the other, because, as I said before, it is death to see the Kareya. Down the hill he came, leading the four blinded men towards me, slowly and stumblingly, as if each moment they would fall and be lamed. When they came to me they set open the sacred blanket, and, feeble as I was, a mere skeleton, nothing but bones and shrivelled skin, they set me on it, and, led by my guide, carried me slowly into the village. All was silent. A few men I saw face downwards in the dust. There was nothing to show that the village was peopled; but I knew that, though I could see them not, and they could not see me, there were hundreds in the wigwams, crouching and waiting for the sacred fire. I brought no fire with me. I had nothing but my skeleton and my thoughts. They carried me, wondering and expecting much, to the assembly chamber dug deep in the ground, and they set me on what they said was the sacred stool on which Kareya sits. Then I waited for the wisdom; but none came. They told me to make the sacred fire; and I waited, but none came. Then they told me to make it again, and they gave me tinder and flints, and told me the fire was the same as other fire, and I was to make it in the same way. So I chipped, and at last the spark fell into the tinder, and I nourished it into a blaze, and the fire was alight, and the smoke rose through the roof. My companion shouted, and the blindfolded men tore off their bandages, and gave me food. And when I had finished eating, a cry went up from my guide, and with a roar and a whoop of joy the warriors swarmed out round the assembly house, all dressed in their finest and best, their trappings, and beadery, and strings of the red scalps of the woodpeckers, which serve amongst us for money. A few had the cherished black deerskin, and those that had not had the head and skin of some other deer stuffed and borne on a staff, the skins flowing loose. Then they all formed a circle and joined in the chant, and the long step dance, lifting and lowering the one foot while they sang, for two hours. All this time the warriors only sang; those that looked on were silent until the sacred dance ended, and then all joined in and danced and sang till they were tired. Then all was over, and I was the Kareya Indian; but I learnt nothing of the knowledge I expected. And when I got strong again, I asked my guide about the meaning of all that had been done, and he could not tell me. And I asked if all that was told was true, and he said he did not know. And I asked who it was that knew the true secrets of our race; and I was told that those only knew the mysteries who had crossed the valley of the Amargosa, where our sacred axe was found. The axe was of green stone, the same stone as you showed me at M'Quarrie's. I asked further about this stone, and I was told that no man knew whence it came, but that fully finished axes were found

on the western slope of the valley. I was told that the
valley was all black rock, and that no green rock was
there, nor was there any such known anywhere except
in the shape of axeheads. Inquiring further into these
things, I was told that those who passed through the
valley learnt all knowledge ; and I resolved to go. The
sacred council tried to stop me ; they said I must not leave
them ; they told me my going meant my death. I asked
them if it was true about the valley, and they said it
was ; and then I warned them I should go. I was
watched night and day ; but I felt angry that the people
should be in darkness, and I made up my mind to find
out the truth, and tell them. And one night I slipped
away. I went to the valley ; and, when I saw the birds
fall as they strove to fly over it, and the waggon stop as
it strove to drive through it, I understood that it was
indeed the Valley of Death, and that the meaning of our
wise men was that they knew nothing. This did not
satisfy me, and I tried to go down in search of the axes ;
and, instead of the axes, I found a nest of the green
stone enough to make axes for an army ; and you too saw
a nest of it on the other side. And so I found that all
the knowledge I had gained was the knowledge that I
knew nothing. And I would have gone back to my
people ; but the council had proclaimed me an outcast,
and sent from tribe to tribe the news that I had been
false to my trust, and that I must die. And all the
Kahrocs and all the Meewocs, and all their allies on this
side of the Sierras, agreed to kill me. But I did not know
that any besides the Kahrocs would do so ; and I came
to work in the land of the Meewocs. The head tribe of
the Meewocs are these Awahnees, and Tenaya, the chief,

is glad to show his power. So he came at night and seized me, and carried me here to sacrifice me to-morrow, that the tribes may tell how the Awahnee chief avenged the treason of the lost Kareya.'

Anything more unexpected than this strange story I could not conceive. It was so utterly different to anything I had imagined, that I was completely taken aback. Ned's facial play was quite a study. Owyanu evidently told the truth, but the thought and action throughout seemed quite opposed to all Indian nature.

'What is your name?' asked Reid.

'Owyanu.'

'Who were your father and mother?'

'My father was Kusudah, and my mother was Muoro.'

'Were both of them natives of your village, or did they come from afar?'

'They were born in our village.'

I rose and looked out through the entrance, and saw Awuyah advancing, waving the branch of truce.

'I come for your answer to Tenaya.'

'What is it to be, Ned?' said I.

'I will go,' said Owyanu. 'You shall not risk your lives to save mine.'

'Will you stand by us to the end, if we stand by you?' asked Ned.

'I will; but it is better I should go.'

'I think not. Tell him we'll fight.'

'Awuyah!' I shouted.

'I am waiting for your answer. The time is passing.'

'Let it pass. This is our answer to Tenaya. Tell him we mean to stay here and to fight; and, as the grizzly rose from its lair to save the outcast from his pursuers, so will

we bar the way to all that come against him. Go back
in safety, but the next man that appears round that rock
shall die; and the next, and the next!'

With a scornful laugh, Awuyah goes back; and, just
as he reaches the buttress, round come Tenaya and his
tribe. With a whoop and a chorus of yells that echo
again and again, as the sound-waves strike the parallel
cliffs, the Awahnees come on to the attack. The
arrows rain round us. Throwing away their bows, the
foremost Indians charge up to storm our stronghold hand
to hand. The moonlight is thinning into the grey of the
morning as that furious crowd, like so many maniacs,
rages up to the door. We fire—and neither misses—and
we pick up the revolvers. But to stop that storm is
hopeless. Bang! bang! bang! go the pistols, but the
advance is unchecked. At the head of his men comes
Tenaya. In a minute he will be in! All seems lost!

When—without a word of warning, without a note of
fear—everything, above, beneath, around, begins to shake.
There is a rattling roar that drives the very cliffs apart.
Tenaya opens his arms to stay his men; and, as our last
shots speed, the light fades, and the fight ends. We
are alone. All is silent as death. We are under an
avalanche!

CHAPTER VII.

UNDER THE SNOW.

OWYANU was the first to break the silence.

'I am sorry.'

'Sorry for what?' asked Reid. 'That we are alive?'

'No. That you should be doomed to a death like this for having helped me.'

'I was thinking we were precious lucky to be saved from a death like that.'

'But we are under the snow!'

'And so is Tenaya, I hope. Keep your eye on the doorway, Langham, in case any of those Diggers should try to wriggle in.'

'I think they all escaped.'

'More's the pity! Let us hope they think we are done for!'

'I am afraid we shall be if help doesn't come soon. And how we are to be found under the snow, I don't quite see.'

'Cheer up,' said Ned. 'After Owyanu's story I am prepared for anything.'

'Well, we must take it coolly.'

'Why, certainly we shall, if we don't have a fire.'

'We cannot have a fire.'

'Why not ?'

'There's no draught; we are all shut in. What will you do with the smoke ?'

'We must have a look as the light gets better. Let us see if our rear is all right.'

And, while I guarded the door, Ned went into the second chamber to find that all was safe.

'Nothing there,' he said, as he came back. 'Let us have something to eat. Where is the cold venison ?'

This he found, and in the darkness we ate in silence.

'No Indian will come to us through the snow,' said Owyanu. 'We could sleep in peace.'

'That's what I was thinking,' said Ned. 'We are all right at present, but we are tired out. Let us have a rest, and when we wake we can talk matters over.'

And we lay down. I made myself comfortable, full length across the doorway. Ned slept across the passage between the inner and outer rooms. The Indian was in the first chamber, between us. I slept for some hours. When I opened my eyes, the sun had evidently risen, for the light was stronger and more diffused. In the pearly gloom I saw Owyanu sitting gazing fixedly at the door. Then he rose and felt the roof with his hands. He was, as I have said, magnificently built, and his fine, powerful figure showed off to perfection, for the Awahnees had stripped him of his working clothes, and all he now wore was his hip-cloth and buckskin girdle. He stood there in the milky light that streamed in through the snow above the breastwork behind me, and as his limbs outlined them-

selves against the sombre background, he seemed to be
holding up the roof, under which his height made him
stoop. The whole weight seemed upon him.

At first I thought I was dreaming, and it was only
gradually that I became aware I was awake. ·

'Well, Owyanu?' I said. 'What are you coing?'

'I think the snow overhead is thin, but it is deep at

the door.   I think we might take away that breastwork
and let in more light.'

'We will wait to hear what Reid says when his sleep
is over.'

'Which it is,' said Ned, rising.   'We can bring those
stones in, and dig away some of the snow.   The more we
get out into it, the more air and light we shall get.'

'Owyanu says the snow overhead is not very thick.'

'How do you know that?   Is that one of the
mysteries?'

'No.   I only think so.   The stream is still running.
It has not been choked.'

'Yes, I suppose we shall be all right for air as long as
that stream runs.'

'Is this stone overhead the only one, or is there another
on the top of it?'

'There is a heap of rubbish there; but in the next
room there is a crack that was open.'

'Let us have the front clear,' said I.

And in a very few minutes our breastwork was down,
and the dim light shone in through the doorway.   Then,
with his knife, Ned carved away at the snow, and we
carried through to the stream all that we dug out.   The
snow was dry and clean as we worked into it, and came
down readily, so that in an hour's time we had an alcove
from the door about a yard and a half in length.

'Driving an adit,' said Ned.   'We expected to go in
for the alluvial, and here we are, landed as soft quartz
crushers.'

This working in the ghastly whiteness of the snow had
a strange effect upon me.   I became quite dazed.   The
cruel glare gave our eyes no rest.   In the cold stillness

our voices sounded hollow and unnatural. Our flesh was
bloodless and pallid. Our clothes seemed to hang on us
like dank, dirty rags.

'You would think,' said I, 'that we were only the
ghosts of ourselves.'

'What does it matter if we are?' answered Ned. 'We
may be, for all you know. But if we can work together
as ghosts the same as we work together as men, what
difference does it make to us?'

'Not the ghost of a difference, I suppose I ought to
say.'

'Then don't bother your head with what you look like,
or what you feel like. Stick to the work that comes along,
and keep your eyes open.'

'Like the coyote,' said Owyanu.

'Like an intelligent man,' said Reid. 'But I suppose
the coyote means much the same thing.'

'I think so, sometimes, but some men are better.'

'Eh? Let us knock off work and take a meal. And
if you don't mind telling us some of that wisdom of the
Kahrocs that ended in nothing, Langham and I will listen.
Why should we keep our eyes open like the coyote?
The reason may give us a notion. Sometimes two trails
are better than one. We are in for a long stay, I expect,
so take your time. There's no hurry.'

'The wisdom of the white man is not the same as that
of the Kahroc.'

'Perhaps not, but it often ends where yours did.'

'The white man laughs at all wisdom but his own.'

'So does the red man.'

'Not always,' said Owyanu; 'but I will tell you the
story I was thinking of. The wise men of the Kahrocs say

that once there was no world. And Kareya sat on the sacred stool, and said to himself he would make one. And first he made the water; and then he made the land. And then he made the fishes that swim in the big water. And then he made the snakes; and then he made the birds; and then he made the animals that walk on the green land. And all the animals were equal, and it was not settled which should be meat for each, and which should be meat for man. Now one evening all the animals were gathered together in a certain place. It was many summers ago, and Kareya had told the man to make bows and arrows of differing length and strength, and give them to the animals as he pleased, according to the power he thought they deserved. The sun had set, and the man, according to Kareya's command, began to make the bows. And it was nine sleeps before the work was ended. And all the animals that were gathered together went to sleep; all but the coyote, who was exceeding cunning, and who said to himself, The man will give the longest bow to him who is first awake. So he laughed to himself, and laid his long nose on his paws, and made believe to be asleep, · like all the others. Now about midnight he himself began to get sleepy; and he scratched his eyes and walked about, and skipped and jumped to keep himself awake. While he was jumping about he woke some of the others; but he soon lay down again, and so did they. Well, he could not keep awake, try all he could, and when the morning star came up, he found he must go to sleep; for the night was so long. So he took two sticks and sharpened them, and with them propped up his eye-lids, so as to take a wink or two while gazing at the morning star. Now he fell quite off to sleep, and the pointed sticks slipped in and pinned his eyelids together. And day broke, and all the birds began to sing, and all the animals went forth to meet the man. And the man gave the longest bow to the cougar, and one by one he gave away the bows, until he was left with the shortest bow of all; and there was none to claim it. So he called over all the animals, and the one that did not answer was the sleeping coyote. And when he looked for him he found him with his eyelids fast together; and, he laughed. But he liked the coyote, and, although he had to give him the shortest bow, he gave him the gift of being ten times more cunning than he had been before. So the coyote is the most cunning of all the animals.'

'I suppose that means,' said I, 'that by keeping our eyes open we shall always learn, but we shall not always prosper.'

'It is a good story,' said Ned, 'and it ought to be of help to us, but I do not yet see how. Do you mean to tell us that those dirty Digger fellows that swarm on the San Joaquin can tell stories like that?'

'They are but Meewocs. I am a Kahroc.'

'Just so. But can all the Kahrocs tell us how the world was made?'

'Only those who are taught by the wise.'

'Oh yes, I forgot,' said Reid. 'What did you mean by keeping our eyes open like the coyote?'

'I meant we might fail, though we might learn much. The Awahnees will watch us from a distance, and in the end we shall fall.'

'Now I am not so sure of that,' said Ned. 'If the Awahnees cannot get at us, the longer we stay here the better, but we must make ourselves comfortable. If we had a coyote here he might dodge up a fire perhaps, for we want one badly. I did not quite see how the bow business bore on our present state; but if you can give us a fire story we might find it useful.'

'It was the coyote who first brought fire to man.'

'Now we are on the track,' said I. 'Proceed, Owyanu, and, if you are in need of a text, tell us how he managed matters under the snow.'

'It is a strange story,' said Owyanu.

'Likely enough,' said Ned.

'There was no fire amongst men; and the men tried in vain to obtain it. It was first made by Kareya, and it was kept from the world by three old hags who lived in a wigwam on the top of a high hill. Many trials did the animals make to get it, but all failed, and the three old women kept it to themselves. Man tried often; and at last he sent for the coyote, who put his long nose on the ground, and lay and thought. Then the coyote went out and called the animals together. And all came, from the cougar to the frog; and with them and an Indian he set out to the hill on which the fire was kept. And he left the frog to keep watch at the bottom of the hill, and all the way up the hill he placed the animals in order. The worst runners were placed first, and the cougar, the strongest of the animals, was placed last, on the top of the hill, near the wigwam of the women. And the Indian he hid under the hill. And all the animals in a long row lay down and waited. Then the coyote walked up the hill and knocked at the door of the wigwam. And one of the hags came to the door, and saw but a little coyote. "Good evening," said the coyote. "Good evening," said the old woman. "It is a cold night," said the coyote;

"can you let me in to sit by the fire?" And the old
woman, seeing he was but a little coyote, let him in.
And he lay down by the fire, and put his nose between
his paws and pretended to sleep. But he was awake all
night watching the women, and the women were watching
him. So, next morning, he thanked the women for their
shelter, and ran down the hill to the Indian, and told him
how carefully the women watched the fire. And he said
to the Indian that the next night he would go to the
cabin, and while he was inside the Indian was to attack
it. So the next night, with the animals all placed on
the hill, he walked up to the door of the wigwam, and
knocked. "Good evening," he said. "Good evening,"
said the old woman. "It is a cold night," said the coyote;
"can you let me sit by the fire?" And the old woman,
seeing he was but a little coyote, let him in. And he lay
down by the fire, and put his nose between his paws and
pretended to sleep. But he was awake all the time.
And in the middle of the night the Indian suddenly
attacked the door. And the three women rushed to
defend it. And the coyote caught up a burning stick in
his teeth, and ran off with it out of the other door.
And the hags saw him, and by the sparks they chased
him, and they ran like the wind. And they had almost
caught the coyote when he reached the cougar; and,
throwing the stick to the cougar, he slunk away. And
the hags chased the cougar; and just as they were over-
taking him he threw the stick to the next, who carried
on the fire. And so from animal to animal it was thrown,
until it came to the ground squirrel. And he carried it
so awkwardly that his tail caught fire, and the pain was
such that he curled his tail up against his back, and so

burned the black spot you see between his shoulders to-day. And the ground squirrel was nearly caught by the hags, and was only just in time to pass on the fire to the next animal. And on it went, from the next to the next, until it came to the frog. And the frog opened his mouth and swallowed the fire and jumped. And one of the hags was so close behind that she caught hold of his tail. And the tail came off in her hands; and no full-grown frog has a tail to this day. So the frog escaped; for he jumped into the water. And he swam under the water for a long way, until he came up out of breath and spit the fire on to a log of driftwood. And the man took the driftwood and dried it in the sun, and when he rubbed it together the fire came forth.'

'Which it would have done without the coyote,' said I, 'had the Indian only had the sense to try.'

'Why, then, we are as bad as the Indian,' said Ned. 'We have been waiting for the fire to come down the hill, and never tried for ourselves. Let us strike a light, and see what we have got to burn.'

And in a minute Reid had a match alight, and was peering round the inner chamber.

'There is wood,' said Owyanu. 'The rock has fallen on trees and bushes. Look!'

Another match held where the Kahroc pointed showed us two or three twigs sticking out from under a lump of stone. In an instant Owyanu had seized the stone and dragged it into the opening. Beyond it were two small blocks, one on the other. He seized the top one, and brought it in. A draught of air blew out the match.

'Swallowed by the frog,' said Ned. 'Here, hold it while I light it.'

Again the light shone in the opening. Owyanu lugged in the lower stone, and Reid, with his hunting-knife, cut at the branch on which they had rested. The light again went out, but Owyanu and Reid seized hold of the branch and dragged at it. It moved a few inches, and we heard something fall, and then it broke off at the cut, and was dragged into the chamber. It was dry.

'Light it,' said Reid.

And we broke it up, and we lit it. And the firelight shone down the opening from which it had come. Along it was a pile of rubbish, and overhead was a huge slab, supported on large stones at the side, one of which was three and the other four feet high. The rubbish was loose, and Owyanu, stooping to the work, threw it back to us in handfuls. The more he cleared, the stronger blew the draught and the worse became the smoke.

'Heed not the smoke,' said Owyanu. 'I see daylight and hear the falling waters.'

Faster flew the rubble towards the fire, and soon the passage was clear. Scrambling over the trunk of a tree, we found ourselves in a third chamber, in which one solid mass of rock leant against another. And through the narrow angle on the right, and from a small gap overhead, the light streamed in.

I ran to the upright mass, and looked through the gap above me. It was the side of the precipice, which towered up straight for hundreds of feet. The snow had fallen clear of the base of the cliff. There was no way out of our prison. But we had found fresh air.

G

CHAPTER VIII

A SURPRISE.

AND so we proceeded to 'make ourselves comfortable.' At first we were doubtful about the fire, but Ned decided it was worth the risk, as it might serve as a signal to M'Quarrie's men, should they find their way to us. We therefore moved into the third chamber, and lighted the fire at the base of the cliff.

We had light, and we could hear the sound of the distant cascades; but we could see only a few yards up the valley. Nearly all the terrors of our imprisonment had, however, vanished. We had food for a fortnight at the least, and by that time we should probably have cut our way out through the snow. Would the Awahnees be in waiting to receive us? Would they dig in to us?

Ned thought they would.

'These Awahnees,' he said, 'were willing to sacrifice everything for the lost Kareya. Most of them evidently looked upon him as accursed. Their attack ended so strangely that they would take the fall of the snow as a judgment. If we were to be quiet they would fancy we were all dead. But still they would watch till the snow melted, in order to make sure. If we keep the fire going, they are bound to see it, and they will watch us night and day. But they will watch us at a safe distance, as they do not like what they call medicine. Now I know that Caffrey will reach the valley, and when he does they will have enough to do to look after themselves; and when he settles them, as he is sure to do, they will tell him about the avalanche, and we shall be got out. What we have to do is to dig just far enough through the snow to be safe, and then watch and wait.'

We therefore lighted up our fire, cooked our dinner, and prepared for a fortnight's rest. For reasons that will be obvious to those acquainted with Indians, we occupied separate rooms. To Owyanu we left the third chamber, and Ned and I occupied the first alternately, the central one being reserved for the man off duty.

It was strange to live in silence under the snow; but it was the only thing we could do. The blocks of which our stronghold was composed were nearly all of giant size, quite beyond our powers to move. We tried to clear a way all round, as we had done through over the tree, but in each case we were stopped before we had proceeded a yard or so. A whole corner of the cliff seemed to have fallen, and the blocks, being shaped by the joint planes and mostly unbroken, were immense, and formed an impassable cage. Fortunately they had fallen upon a clump of trees and underwood, so that there was no want of fuel.

Thanks to the light in the third cave, we could tell the duration of the night and day, and regulate our work and leisure. The work was simple enough ; all we had to do was to dig out the snow in front of the door and drive the gallery towards the valley. How many tons of snow we cleared out and melted in the middle cave, I am afraid to say, as, calculating the quantity cut and carried each hour by the number of hours we were at work, the total amounts to too many tons to be easily credible. And I have no wish to exaggerate, or to make any statements that may cast a doubt on the truth of this straightforward story of facts.

On the second morning after our imprisonment, we were called by Owyanu to listen at our peep-hole. Above the murmur of the waterfalls we could hear what seemed to be the report of firearms. At first these sounds were distant, but they gradually approached, and then died away again. All was silent for a time, and then a confused murmuring smote on our ears, and Reid said he could distinguish the gallop of horses. Perhaps he could ; perhaps he could not. At any rate, the noise all died away, and we heard no more than the monotonous water music. In the hope that our friends had come, we made up the fire so as to give as much smoke as possible. But we waited for succour in vain. Nothing came, and we watched anxiously all that night and the next day, and kept the fire going to no purpose. This was a great disappointment to us. However, we agreed that we must have been mistaken, and that we had only to wait a little longer for relief.

Our next adventure, if adventure it can be called, was about a week afterwards, at supper - time. We were silently munching away at our venison, when we heard a peculiar rattle, and, before we could move, a lithe body glided from Reid's legs and disappeared through one of the crevices between the rocks.

'A rattlesnake!' exclaimed Reid; 'rather too near to be pleasant! I wonder whether there are any more of them!'

'They will not hurt you,' said Owyanu.

'I am not so sure of that.'

'The serpent will never hurt you so long as you carry that piece of green stone with you.'

'Is that so?' asked Ned.

'It is. The serpent fears the sacred stone.'

'Have you a piece with you?'

'I have.'

'Then, Langham, I'll give you half mine, and we shall all three be rattlesnake-proof.'

'The stone must be unbroken as it comes from the valley.'

'Then I'm sorry. You are out of it, old chap.'

'Oh, don't apologize!' I said; 'I'll take my chance. But is there any connection between the snake and the stone?'

'The snake is sacred. In the south-east of the mountains they worship him, and there they keep the implements of stone.'

'Oh yes, I remember!' said Ned. 'I have heard that somewhere on the Rio Grande they have a snake dance every year.'

'They have, at Hualpi.'

'Are the dancers of the same tribe as yours?'

'No; they are the Opeyai, who live near the people whose hawks come to the finger, tamed and trained to prey for the villagers. The white men call them Moquis. And each year, on the ninth day before our Kareya goes forth to fast, they hold their solemn festival and worship the serpents and the implements of stone.'

'Were you ever there?'

'No; but those who have seen it have told me. On their altar they heap the stalks of ripening corn, and in front of the corn they lay the calumets, and behind them they pile the axes, hoes, and trowels. Many of the axes are of slate, many more of obsidian, like that which lines the Amargosa, and many more are of the green stone.'

'But they don't really worship the rattlesnake?'

'Yes, worship the rattlesnake. They gather the snakes and charm them, and join with them in the dance.'

'Join with them in the dance!'

'They charm the snakes and coax them with the feather wand. And they carry the snakes in their left hands, and in their right hands, and in their mouths. They march, and dance, and prance with the snakes, which fondle and obey them.'

'But the poison fangs are taken out?'

'No; the poison is there, but the snake dare not break the charm of the mighty medicine. The dance is a great sight to see. The men wear their serpent cloths and scarlet moccasins, and make themselves gay with broad white armlets and yellow skins of the fox; their hair is made bright with the tufts of the woodpecker, and their faces are blackened to 'their lips, and whitened to their necks, and in the mouth, where the black line meets the white line, they hold the rattle of the writhing snake.'

'But what is the end of all this?' asked I, in amazement.

'The snakes are sprinkled with the sacred meal, and picked up by the children and passed on to the chief, who prays over them, and herds them in the circle by the sacred rock. And when they have all been gathered, the meal is sprinkled on the heap, and then the men rush on to them, grasp them in handfuls, and run to the east and down the cliff, and throw them to the winds.'

'Do you mean to say Indians grasp handfuls of live rattlesnakes and scatter them broadcast over the country?'

'They do.'

'Where?'

'Far over the mountains in the plains to the northeast, in Hualpi, Tegua, and Suchongnewy, the villages of the Opeyai.'

'How horrible!' said I.

'Your Indian religions, Owyanu,' said Ned, 'are not very comforting. The lesson you learnt by your trip to the Death Valley was not a cheering one. And nothing you have told us, or hinted to us, seems to hold out any hope for you.'

'I am but a poor Indian.'

'Then why remain so? Why not have some of the white man's faith?'

'The faith of the white man is not for the Indian.'

'If faith is good for any, it is good for all.'

'Even for the little coyote?'

Ned was rather staggered.

'Well, yes, even for the coyote.'

'It is not so,' said Owyanu. 'The Indian can never be like the white man. The chance came to him, and stayed with him for a while; and now it has gone, and the Indian must die.'

'Nonsense, man! Listen to the white man's faith! You may miss ninety-nine chances, but save yourself with the hundredth.'

'It is better for all men that faith did not save the coyote; it is better for the white man that faith does not save the Indian!'

'One would think you were old M'Quarrie!'

'It is true! The Indian's time is past, and you can only whisper in his ear the message of those that have gone before him to the plains beyond the Western Sea, from whence he came. Lay him in the ground, hang up his clothes above him, and let the shells over his grave go clicking and chattering in the night wind, while no one speaks his name. Here the white man rules; there the Indian has another chance!'

Let it not be supposed that I give the exact words of Owyanu. His phrases had all the meaning I have tried to give them, but the words were often absurdly ill-chosen and the structure of the sentence ungrammatical. To give the exact words would, however, be painful to me, and I do not care to burlesque his speech by sprinkling it with errors and curiosities.

'Then it comes to this, Owyanu: we must do our work well, no matter who's the master or what's the pay?'

'Work and help; and you white men work for your race, and not for yourselves as we poor Indians did.'

'We are getting down to the usual pegging away.'

'Yes, pegging away like Tutakanoola.'

'What was that gentleman's name?' I asked.

'Tutakanoola.'

'Who was he?'

'Long, long ago two little boys were playing in the Wakalla. They bathed and swam, and splashed each other. And then they were tired, and they climbed on to a stone by the stream, and fell asleep side by side in the sun. And as soon as they fell asleep the stone began to rise, for the stone was the top of a mighty rock. And inch by inch the rock rose to the sky. And the fathers and mothers sought the boys in vain, for they were on the top of the rock and no one could see them there. The sun went down, and the moon passed over, and still the rock rose, until at last it reached the sky, and, as the moon rolled across, it touched the boys' faces with its edge. Now, although the Indians knew not what had become of the boys, the animals did. And they all gathered together in this valley; and, because the boys had been good to them and not hurt them, they resolved to bring them home again. And the boys still slept, and the rock stopped rising. Then it was agreed that the animals should spring to the top of the rock one after the other. And first the mouse sprang, and he jumped but a handbreadth. And then the rat jumped, and he jumped two handbreadths. And all tried, one after the other, and none reached near the top. And the highest jump was that of the grizzly bear, and when he failed the animals all gave up. But before they had gone away there came along

Tutakanoola, the little measuring-worm, which even the mouse could have crushed had she trodden on him. And they told Tutakanoola why they were there, and how they had failed. And Tutakanoola said he would bring down the boys. And all the animals laughed. And the little measuring-worm crept to the foot of the cliff, and began to creep up it. And he crept past the jump of the mouse, and past the jump of the rat, and at last past the jump of the grizzly bear. Very slowly up he went till he was out of sight. But though no one was looking, he still kept on, although he was but a little measuring-worm. And up he went to the very top, and found the children; and there strength was given him because he had succeeded, and he brought the children down. But the rock remains to this day, and it is the seventh peak from this on the side of the valley below the great cascade.'

'Talk about philosophy from a brazen image!' said Reid. 'That's just the sort of story my father used to read out to us! Have you any more of the same sort?'

And then Owyanu told us another and then another of his wondrous store of Indian legends and fables. I fancy I can see him now, sitting there in the firelight, with his piercing eyes shining like diamonds as the reflection of the flame shot across them.

'It's all very well for you to talk to us about Kahrocs and Meewocs and such people,' said Reid to him; 'but you will never make me believe you are a thoroughbred Indian. I never saw or heard of such a redskin before. You must have been changed at nurse, shipwrecked when a boy, or something of the sort. The only Indian thing about you is the bronze varnish you wear. You are no more a Digger than I am a born backwoodsman.'

'But you are going to stay in the backwoods, are you not?' asked I.

'Ah, I suppose so! I wonder how that gravel pit is getting on!'

'And I wonder. Let us refresh ourselves with a peep at the mystic document.'

And I flattened it out on my knee, and we read it over again together. And then we turned it over and studied the map.

That was a map; or rather it is, for I have it with me now! There are rivers and there are branches, but the rivers and the branches are all of the same thickness, and run at right angles to each other; and, as there are no other marks but circles and crosses, and no indication as to which is the north of the map, the opportunity it offered for mental recreation may be imagined. We marked the sides 1, 2, 3, and 4. I felt sure that 1 was the northern side; Ned insisted that that must be the eastern side, 'towards the morning.' Turn the map as we would, neither I nor Ned nor Owyanu could make out the least resemblance between it and the Awahnee valley.

We had told Owyanu how Taipoksee had said that the gold came from the home of the Awahnees, but he did not seem to take the remark in the same spirit that we had done.

'You say I am no Indian; but Taipoksee is not so much of an Indian. If he knew where the gold came from, he would go there to fetch it.'

'Perhaps it would not be worth his while.'

'It is not worth his while. It comes a little at a time down each of these streams, and down all the streams that join the Wakalla.'

' That's it, I believe ; and where his village is, the fall and the bed of rock are so arranged that the lighter sand and stone are dashed out and along into the stream, while the heavier gold is caught in the hollow.'

' Then you'll have to buy out Taipoksee !' laughed Reid.

' And of course, as you are my partner, you'll find half the funds ! '

The more we thought of our golden gravel, the more we made fun of it, and the less and less grew the chance of our making a serious effort to obtain it. A fortnight passed, and .we still worked onwards at our gallery, and no help had come. Latterly we had dug on very slowly and cautiously, and with a due regard to our defence in the event of the enemy breaking in. We had thought best to keep on the ground, and not attempt to get to the light upwards, as we should certainly have fallen an easy prey to the Awahnees had we been caught struggling out of the snowdrift. How thick the snow was we had no means of knowing, but from the terrible force of the blow we suspected that the mass must be enormous. As it happened, we went the longest way to work ; but it was the safest. As we had to command the approach to the caves, our gallery had to be straight, and the straight line, as luck would have it, led directly through the greatest length of the avalanche.

The first night of our captivity was a very cold one, and the frost lasted for a week ; but during the second week a gradual thaw set in, and the stream running through the central cave became much larger. It seemed as though we should be thawed out before we were helped out. The prospect was not an inviting one. We pretended to be exceedingly cheerful, but our cheerfulness got hollower and hollower during the second week. In our hearts we were growing tired of our make-believe.

'We shall have to end this thing,' said Reid on the sixteenth day, as he contemplated the remainder of the deer; 'we shall be starved out.'

Not a sound was there but the ceaseless murmur of the waterfalls. Although we watched and listened, not a whisper could we hear, not a sign of man or his works did either of us discover.

The next morning we held a serious consultation as to what was best to be done. After going through the question in all its bearings, we agreed to begin energetic action. We were to cut our way out through the gallery, but if possible to keep a thin veil at the end to be broken through at night. And we were then to attempt a retreat up the canyon. We did not like giving up the gold, the horses, or our friends; but we saw no other way of saving our lives.

'If we must die,' said Reid, 'let us die in the daylight.'

And so we started on our final effort. Owyanu cut out the snow, I carried it to the cave, and Reid stood armed and ready in case the figure of an Awahnee showed itself through the wreath.

About eleven o'clock, while I was in the central cave, I heard a sound of footsteps. I gave the alarm, and we ceased working, and speedily made ourselves ready for a desperate rush for freedom.

The footsteps drew nearer, and we heard men's voices. Strange voices they were, seemingly Indians' voices, but all was so indistinct that we could distinguish nothing.

In about a quarter of an hour we could hear that there were several people gathered round us. The sound was reflected by the cliff. Were the speakers friends or foes? One thing was certain—they were Indians.

Suddenly there came a grating, rattling noise. The people were moving on the top of the granite blocks! We looked at each other in dismay. The snow had evidently gone from above. The noise came directly overhead.

'They are moving to the door,' whispered Reid. 'They will drop in front of it.'

'The roof is thin,' said Owyanu. 'Stand clear of the steps, the roof may fall in !'

The footsteps softly and stealthily gathered overhead.

'Moccasins !' said Owyanu ; 'not boots !'

Suddenly there was a shout. Then came a shower of snow down the doorway. The light broke in at the same moment as a figure fell to the ground.

Up went Reid's rifle ; but Owyanu struck the barrel aside. The figure gathered itself together briskly, stood for an instant in the full light of the sun against the background of the long white tunnel, and stepped into the cave with,—

'How do, Ned Reid ! Me friend in need !'

'Why !' said Ned,—'why — why !—it's — it's — it's young Bearspaw !'

CHAPTER IX.

THE ROAD HOME.

BEARSPAW followed his son, and in a few seconds half a dozen of his following had dropped into our tunnel and began to clear it from the top. The snow roof was hardly a foot thick, and the passage was soon laid open. We were free.

But where were our companions? Where were the Awahnees? How had Bearspaw, of all men, sprung upon us in this strange fashion?

Of our greetings I say nothing. An Indian's greeting is not a very gushing affair. And Bearspaw was an Indian of the true type, there could be no doubt of that. To Reid he was friendly, to me he was dignified, to Owyanu he was as indifferent as if he had been with him for months. The youngster really gave us the best welcome. He was evidently mightily pleased at his lucky tumble into the doorway, and it was only the thought of his father's presence that kept him from exuberance.

Bearspaw's story was short and to the point. He was not a great orator in the English tongue, but he had a knack of packing an immense amount of meaning into the most excruciating fragments of phrases.

It seemed that Bearspaw had been hired, with his men, as guides and escort to a body of emigrants bound for California, who had got seriously wrong as to their route in the plains. Luckily for them, and for Bearspaw, they happened to be sighted by that active warrior when they were uncertain what to do next. Bearspaw offered his advice as to the road, and, receiving a fair offer, packed up his few belongings and with them came over the Sierra by the Sonora Pass. At Sonora his contract terminated, and he was on his way back when he happened to meet with some Mono Indians. From them he heard strange tidings.

That very morning they had been joined by a couple of Awahnees asking their protection. These told him how about ten days before they had been driven out of their valley by the white men. These white men were led by a Captain Boling, and Caffrey.

It seemed that Caffrey had been reinforced and started on the trail when he heard of another expedition headed by Captain Boling, one of the settlers farther to the south, who was also in search of missing horses. Boling had been told by Jose Juarez and Cowchitti that the horses had been stolen by Awahnees, and at their instigation he had got together a few friends and pursued. Caffrey, keeping to the south, joined hands with Boling, who took the command. The expedition entered the valley by the southern trail. The Awahnees stood on their defence, called in the men who were watching our cave, and made a grand fight for their own. They were hopelessly beaten, and driven up into the mountains. Not an Indian remained in the valley alive. Boling and Caffrey swept away the horses, and, in fact, made a regular clearance; and, being unable to learn anything of us, had marched back home. But the Awahnees who escaped to the Monos told them the story of the two white men and the lost Kareya so strangely imprisoned in the snow. And they also told them how, when the snow fell upon us, the sacred fire was lighted at the foot of the cliff. Bearspaw, listening to this eventful history, happened to ask for the names of the white men; and the Awahnee, who was no other than our fat friend Awuyah, gave us our full titles of 'the potent signiors of the Western Sea, the Langham and the Reid.'

From the description Awuyah gave, Bearspaw recognised 'the Reid' as his friend Ned; and, thinking that if he had escaped the Death Valley it was rather hard to let him perish under the snow, had parted from the Monos, and then set off direct for the Wakalla.

Thanks to the description given by Awuyah, they had no difficulty in finding the avalanche, or rather its remains, for the thaw had thinned it considerably. It seemed that it was not unusual for avalanches to sweep into the valley from the feeders of the Wakalla, and that ours was not the only one that had fallen. But Bearspaw, entering on the north nearer the ruins of the village, and making his way up to the lake, had rounded the bluff where the fight began, and immediately identified our stronghold. Any doubt he might have had was soon dissipated by the sight

B

of the smoke which suddenly shot up near the cliff.
With all due caution the Indians approached us, and
mounted the roof in the hope of finding their way across
to the door. The snow was then about seven feet thick
on the ground, but the greatest mass had fallen across
the doorway, and overhead only a few inches were left.
Young Bearspaw, boy-like, had been busily prospecting
where nobody else thought of going, and the result was
his sudden disappearance from above, and startling
tumble to the rescue.

When we heard all this it seemed as though an age
had elapsed since we had been shut in. The hope of
eventual release, and the conviction that our best hope
of escaping alive was to take things easily, had led us
to spend the time cheerfully; and the days went
by during the first week almost too quickly for us.
But now we were out, the seventeen days seemed to have
been so many months. While we were under the snow
a kingdom had been invaded, a decisive battle fought, a
nation routed, and driven for ever from their country; and
the conquerors had retired in triumph, leaving a solitude
behind them!

But such a solitude! In the camp we stayed a couple
of days to recover our strength. We spent the time in
wandering about the valley, looking in vain for the golden
gravel, and during our frequent rests listening to Owyanu
as he told us the local legends. Every cliff and waterfall
seemed to have its story. Tutakanoola proved to be the
huge rock that had attracted us so in the moonlight;
Tisseyak was not far from our stronghold, a tremendous
mass nearly five thousand feet high; facing it was another
giant buttress known as Tokoye; down the valley and to

the south of the Wakalla was the church-like group of
Kosuko, with the mighty tower of Sakkadueh.   We had
seen the valley from above in the golden blaze of noon ;
we had seen it from below in the silver radiance of the
moonlight ; we saw it now in all the wealth of the million
hues of the setting sun.   And it is in the sunset, with its
cliffs and cataracts aglow with the colours of fire, that I
still like best to picture it.   It had then an awful beauty;
a beauty that threatened of the night, of the darkness that
was to come.

While the rosy blush of the lingering day was mantling
the rocky ramparts, we wandered down to the chief waterfalls.   We stood in silence by the side of Yowaiyi as she
came leaping, leaping nearer home ; we gazed at the long
veil of Pohono until her witchery fell stealing over us as
it did over the Indian maids ; and we listened to the
roaring melody of Cholok and the flute-like song of Tualpa,
and wondered how Bearspaw and his men could have
found their way by her side without halting to worship.
For it was down her ravine that our rescuers had come.

That evening we watched the reflections fade in the
mirror lake of Awaia ; and next morning at break of day
we were up and making ready for our journey across the
mountains.   Our horses had been snatched away from us ;
we had given up the gold quest in despair ; we had found
and rescued the Barber.   The only thing left to us seemed
to be 'to start afresh,' as Ned said ; and we decided to
accompany Bearspaw on his way back, until, at any rate,
we reached one of the main tracks to the San Joaquin.

I forgot to mention that I had been duly introduced to
Mrs. Bearspaw, who had come with her husband and son.
The good lady was hardly of prepossessing appearance or

conversation ; but she evidently regarded us with no
unfriendly eye, and had promptly classified both Owyanu
and myself in the same category as Ned, as distinguished
from the hapless emigrants. The Bearspaws evidently cared
not a jot for the lost Kareya ; in fact, I have my doubts
if they cared for anything. Perhaps I say so hastily, or
rather ought not to say so at all, for old Bearspaw pre-
sented Owyanu with an old rifle, as, I suppose, a mark of his
esteem ; and he made the gift with the greatest approach
to cordiality I ever saw him manage. I fancy Reid had
something to do with the business, but it is of no impor-
tance. Bearspaw was a very decent fellow, all things
considered, and his failings were those of his race.

, With young Bearspaw—his real name was something
about six inches long, in eight or nine three-lettered
syllables—I became great friends. He was a bright, active
little fellow, always anxious to be doing, and never happy
unless he was in a post of responsibility.   Quick in
comprehension, of rather sensitive nature, trusting and
fearless, he was, as Owyanu said, ' Good Indian ! good
boy ! ' adding, as if in a spirit of prophecy, ' But the best
go first ! '

Bearspaw's route lay through the Sonora Pass, and we
were to go back nearly the way he had come. By eight
o'clock we were on the move down into the valley.   We
took our last look of Tokoye, and its reflection in the
glassy Awaia ; we passed the foot of Cholok, clearing
with difficulty the stream it fed; we bade farewell to
Tutakanoola, and envied the climbing powers of the little
measuring-worm ; and then we toiled up the trail, and as
we rose the valley shut in behind us.   We skirted it for
a little, and then, with a farewell glance, struck off, bound

for the Tuolumne. That night we camped out on the mountains, and the next day we opened up what seemed to be a model of the valley of the Awahnees. There were the river, and the meadows, and the trees, and the cliffs, and the waterfalls, all produced on a smaller scale. Had we seen this valley first, we should have thought it the loveliest in the world. Owyanu told us that it was the vale of Hatchatchee, and that the bold rock that towered above the tall pines and spruces at its foot was the giant Kolana. One of the cascades surpassed in beauty any I ever saw. It was of great height, and just broad enough to be gracefully proportionate; and it was light as a veil, and curved and swung and quivered as it fell.

Instead of descending the Hatchatchee, we kept up along the bank of the Tuolumne. This is the wonderful river that has cut its gorge down into the solid rock for a thousand feet and more, although it is but a hundred feet wide; and it leaps and leaps in cascade after cascade until it falls nearly five thousand feet in two-and-twenty miles. Narrow as is the Tuolumne, it is deep, and the body of water it contains is enormous, as we were soon to know. Following the river we came to another opening of the gorge, another valley, a model of the Hatchatchee, as the Hatchatchee was a model of that of the Awahnees. Into this valley we descended, and we camped there for the night, hushed to sleep, like Roric Mohr, by the lullaby of the falling water.

CHAPTER X.

IN the morning we found that we had not been alone. As we were on our march out of the valley, we overtook an Indian and his squaw, who had pitched their camp some two miles to the east among a pile of stones that lay at the foot of one of the cliffs. For in all respects, as I have said, this valley was the counterpart of that in which we had been imprisoned.

They were Kahrocs on their way to join their tribe on the Sacramento. The Indian had been on a message to Tenaya, but had found the Awahnees dispersed. He had met with some of the Monos, who had told him the story of the strange incident of the avalanche; and he recognised us as the survivors, and made it his business to

inform Bearspaw that Owyanu was the lost Kareya.
Bearspaw's indifference stood us in good stead. Without
the slightest sign of interest he remarked that he was
aware of the fact, and that Owyanu was his friend.
Ahma stood rebuked; but he joined our company. He
was evidently biding his time.

So thought we all. Mrs. Bearspaw eyed the new-comer
from head to foot, and sniffed her disapproval. She gave
the tone to our society. Bearspaw himself seemed
gradually to awake to the knowledge that Ahma knew
the trail better than he did, and it would be more con-
venient for everybody if he kept in front. And his men
took the hint. Reid whispered that we had better look
out.

'Mischief brewing.'

Young Bearspaw and Owyanu were side by side.

'Him bad man,' said the youngster. 'Him kill you.'

'No,' said Owyanu. 'He cannot, and he will not. He
dare not. But he will crow when I am dead, and say he
did it.'

Slowly we toiled up the ravine.

'There are no more valleys,' said Owyanu.

'Then let us take a last long look at this one,' said I.

And we turned to the left and made our way to the
edge of the precipice.

We were on a sort of promontory where a huge buttress of granite jutted into the plain 1800 feet below.
Owyanu and young Bearspaw were in front. Then came
Reid and I. Close to us were Bearspaw and his men.
Behind us were Ahma and his wife. The Indians seemed
to care nothing for the view; they stood there listless
and indifferent,—all but Bearspaw, who kept his hand

on his rifle and his eye on the Kahroc; and the Kahroc, who seemed to watch us all as if he were a snake.

The atmosphere was thick and oppressive. Not a breath of air was stirring. The river sighed as it flowed, and the cascades hung heavily. The sun was like a globe of fire.

Suddenly the water seemed to change to oil; the current stopped; the river rose. And then, with a roar that deafened us, so that our ears for a time were as dead, the ground shook beneath our feet. We fell prone, and lay there as the cliff top pitched and rolled like the deck of a ship at sea. At the first shock the rock was split in two, and the crag fell inwards to the valley. On it were young Bearspaw and Owyanu! In horror, as we heaved and swayed, we saw the mass shiver into fragments. The boy fell first; thrown down a crack in the ravine. The man was hurled head foremost far out into the lake.

For as the crag was rent the whole edge of the valley split off from the cliffs, and, crumpling and gaping and cracking, the floor fell in. Down for twenty feet dropped the river bed. Across the throat of the canyon a fissure opened, and a cataract formed where the river a moment before flowed on the level. The cataract only lasted for an instant. The river came with a leap and a rush, as if in triumph, and its flood roared on like a perpendicular wall. Furiously it swept in, carrying everything before it, over the wild confusion of the breaking rocks and writhing trees, and the yawning, crunching, quivering ground.

Awed and helpless, we lay there, watching the deluge as it flowed over what had been one of the fairest valleys of California. Soon the waves licked the base of the cliffs; the new base, that is, for the fall had bared many feet more of the granite scarp. Higher, higher they rose over

the fallen trees, over the fallen blocks. Soon they had
reached the old level of the stream ; and the lower river,

which had run dry for a few minutes, filled up again ;
and all was quiet. The Tuolumne flowed into a lake ;

the lake filled the valley; and the Tuolumne flowed out at its western end.

Ahma was the first to recover himself. As soon as the earthquake ceased, he sprang forward on to the now safe cliff, and, stretching forth his right hand over the lake, yelled out,—

'The curse of the lost Kareya!'

We went back down the ravine; and there, in a rift in the rock, within a yard of the water, lay young Bearspaw, silent and—dead.

His father looked on him seemingly unmoved; his mother gazed in tearful despair. The Kahrocs joined us unnoticed. Ahma blinked away across the wide sheet of water, and said,—

'It came for the bad man! It came for him who betrayed his trust!'

'And that poor boy? What had he done?' asked Ned.

If Ahma was heartless, not so was his wife. She looked at the old chief as his dry eyes rested on his only son; she looked at the mother now bending with grief; she looked at the silent Indians. And then her woman's nature welled up. Perhaps the recollection of those she had lost awoke her sympathy and stirred her heartstrings. A great change came over her; she sobbed and shuddered for a minute or two; and then, with a long wild moan, she broke into a tearful chant, which we afterwards learnt was the death-wail of the Kahrocs. It was but a simple, savage dirge, sung to the murmur of the still restless water and the splash of the cascades as they fell direct into the new lake. The 'wail' was for the benefit of young Bearspaw, but I could not help accepting it as equally Owyanu's farewell.

Raising her hands over her head, and opening them towards the setting sun, the Kahroc sang, now high, now low, now almost in a whisper, now broken with sobs, now in a torrent of tears.

'Oh, darling, my dear one, good-bye, good-bye! Your little hands shall clasp your mother's cheeks—never more! Your little feet shall tread the earth around her cabin—never more! You are going on a long, long journey, away, away, to the distant spirit land. And you must go alone, alone, for none here can go with you. Listen then to the words I tell you, and heed them well, for I speak the truth—the truth. In the far spirit land, my darling, there are two roads for you to go. One of them is strewn with roses, and leads to the happy western land beyond the great water; and there one day you shall find your home. The other is strewn with briars and thorns, and leads, I know not whither, to an evil land, the haunt of the deadly snakes; and there you may wander wearily for ever. Oh, my darling, my dear one! choose you the path of roses that leads to the happy western land; for it is a fair and sunny land, and beautiful as the morning. Your little tender feet must walk the path alone—alone. And may the great Kareya help you and guide your footsteps to the right! Good-bye! good-bye! My darling, my dear one, good-bye!'

We reached Sonora. The shock of the earthquake had been felt there; and the roar as the valley fell in had been heard and wondered at. It was the most awful catastrophe I have seen; never before or since have I felt so powerless in a time of peril. And I have had some experience of danger. Twenty years afterwards I was in the wreck of the *Dashing Spray* when she went down in a cyclone, and we took to a boat, and spent thirty-one days starving on the sea. That was a terrible trial, but it was as nothing compared to what I went through with Ned and Owyanu.

It will be seen that I did not stay in California. I had had enough of it; and I returned to the sailoring. At Sonora I parted with Bearspaw. Reid came with me to San Francisco, and thence went home, for a time at least, to New Orleans.

Now I find that the home of the Awahnees has become a public park, or something of the sort, and that it has been rechristened after the grizzly that came to our rescue in the moonlight. 'Uzumaitee! Uzumaitee!' has been transmogrified into Yo Semiteh, and further clipped into Yosemite.

And I hear that Professor Whitney and the Californian geologists now affirm that, as the lake was formed by the earthquake, so was Tahoe, and so were all these valleys at first formed by the in-fall of their beds.

Further, as the curious reader may discover for himself on tracing up the course of the Tuolumne from its junction with the San Joaquin, the Hatchatchee now figures on the map in some corruption. And a few miles to the east of it, in lat. 37° 50′ N., long. 119° 30′ W., the lake we saw made now bears the name of Owyanu, the lost Kareya.

MORRISON AND GIBB, EDINBURGH,
PRINTERS TO HER MAJESTY'S STATIONERY OFFICE.

E46124687964.

www.ingramcontent.com/pod-product-compliance
Lightning Source LLC
Chambersburg PA
CBHW020801020726
47495CB00008B/2532